His mom cocked her head in thought. "Dakota, there was a little girl, a long time ago."

She paused and studied her son. "She was very special to you."

His eyes widened. The past came flooding back. He remembered something in grade school. A playground and this little blond-haired girl. "Was it Mary, Margaret…" he said. "Meghan!" He shook his head in disbelief. He hadn't thought of her in ages. "Could it be? It's been something like twenty years. I wouldn't know her. She wouldn't know me."

It couldn't be her, he thought. What would she be doing back here in Shenandoah? "Last I heard, her family had moved to Fort Worth."

"Well," his mother said, "whether it's Meghan or not, one thing is clear."

"What's that?" Dakota asked, as more and more snatches of memory presented themselves.

"She came to you for help."

Books by Cheryl Wolverton

Love Inspired

Love Inspired Suspense

*Hill Creek, Texas
†Everyday Heroes

CHERYL WOLVERTON

RITA® Award finalist Cheryl Wolverton has well over a dozen books to her name. Her very popular *Hill Creek, Texas,* series has been a finalist in many contests. Having grown up in Oklahoma, lived in Kentucky, Texas, Louisiana and now living once more in Oklahoma, Cheryl and her husband of more than twenty years and their two children, Jeremiah and Christina, always considered themselves Oklahomans transplanted to grow and flourish in the South. Readers are always welcome to contact her at P.O. Box 106, Faxon, OK 73540 or e-mail at Cheryl@cherylwolverton.com. You can also visit her Web site at www.cherylwolverton.com.

HOME TO YOU
CHERYL WOLVERTON

Steeple
Hill®

Published by Steeple Hill Books™

STEEPLE HILL BOOKS

Steeple
Hill®

ISBN 0-373-87344-1

HOME TO YOU

www.SteepleHill.com

Printed in U.S.A.

Fear not for I am with thee: be not dismayed;
for I am thy God: I will strengthen you,
I will help you, yea I will uphold you
with the right hand of my righteousness.
—*Isaiah* 41:10

ACKNOWLEDGMENTS

To my neighbor Melinda
and her wonderful husband and kids. I'll miss you.

To my family, Anita, Doug, Deb, Mom, James
and Gayle. Just for being family.

To my MS support group in Baton Rouge.
Thanks for all the experience. Without you,
I wouldn't have been able to write this book.

And to my wonderful church family,
Cornerstone Fellowship. Jackay and Dick, you are
an inspiration, and I will never forget you or any of
the other wonderful, wonderful friends, especially
Kendal, Lane, Katie, Hope, Claire, Lyndee, Jamie,
Caleb, Jamie, Brooklyn—keepers of my own heart.

When I was going through the discovery of the
MS and the multiple attacks, you guys at church
were there to stand by me and help me through the
day and laugh with me when I couldn't remember
a word or help me when I couldn't walk across
the floor. You are the reason I didn't end up like
Meghan in the book! Such love. God's love.

And of course, Steve, Christina and Jeremiah have
to be added to the list. Being in a family means
good times, bad times and scary times. And we
made it through it. I'm sure more good times, bad
times and scary times will come, but if not for you,
I wouldn't be writing. I love you guys.

And finally, thank You Heavenly Father,
because You *are* in control at *all* times!

Prologue

Dakota "Cody" Ryder sat next to the ditch, watching as his best friend, Meghan O'Halleran, dug some more mud out of the slimy wet pit and slapped it into the pan she had in front of her. It didn't matter that Cody wasn't supposed to get muddy. Sitting with his best friend took precedence over that. Meghan's mom had told her they were moving and so Cody was trying to cheer Meghan up by sitting with her.

"Cody, will you promise me something?"

Dakota was only in first grade, just like Meghan, but he knew what promises were and how important they could be. Last year the two friends had spit in each other's hands and shook, agreeing to protect each other when they started school.

Had they not made that promise, Meghan would have ended up with her hair cut by Michael the bully, and Dakota would have ended up having to work with silly Sally who laughed all the time. Meghan had bailed him out of that one. Big time. Just as he had protected her.

So yes, he knew how important his word was now as Meghan solemnly asked him for another promise.

Her blond hair was pulled up into pigtails, curling tightly, and the freckles across her nose danced as she wriggled it up.

The two friends had helped each other out so many times…but, well, sometimes girls did funny things. So, even though he wanted to promise Meghan the moon, he hesitated as he watched Meghan carefully finish her mud pie. If he promised, he'd have to keep it—no matter what. And if she wanted him to eat that mud pie—

"What do you want me to promise, Meghan?" Cody rested his hands on his crossed legs and waited, trepidation growing as he watched her smooth the top of the pie.

"Promise me we'll always be friends, no matter what."

Relief wilted him. He nodded. "Sure, Meghan!"

"I'm serious. I really mean it, Cody. I want us to always be friends."

"Forever," Cody reassured her. He was so relieved that she didn't want him to eat the pie that he hurried to reassure her. "If you ever need me, I'll be here—even if you want to move in and be my sister."

To Cody that was as good of a promise as he could imagine. He had an older sister and he knew how awful it could be.

Meghan's green eyes peered into his. "Really? Even that? That's great, but I wouldn't want to be your sister."

Cody had shared several stories about his sister with Meghan, and his friend had sometimes caught the wrath of Susan herself, so she knew exactly what Cody was promising.

He nodded. "I promise."

Meghan's lip trembled and her eyes filled with tears.

Suddenly scared, Dakota wondered what he'd said to upset her, until she lunged forward and threw her arms around his neck. "Thank you, Cody! You're the bestest friend ever."

He wrinkled his own nose in disgust. Why'd girls always have to hug?

Then he felt something wet and looked down.

The mud pie was in his lap.

Meghan pulled back and cried in dismay. "I wanted to share it with you before we moved!"

As Cody stared at the mess in his lap and thought of the coming punishment for getting dirty, he could only think he was still getting off a lot easier than he would have if he'd been forced to eat that mud pie.

Chapter One

Thirty-two-year-old Dakota Ryder quickly finished the report he was reading and scrawled his signature across the bottom. He leaned back in the dark brown leather chair, grimacing as he heard it squeak. He needed to get that oiled, he thought, but then immediately dismissed the idea as yet another thing to do later, when he had more time. He glanced at the clock over the sofa and sighed. Pushing back from his mahogany desk, he grabbed up the papers he'd just finished and stood. He was running late.

He strode across the deep, thick, mauve carpet, pausing only to pull open the door before leaving his office. At Sherry Anne's desk, his assistant, who was busily creating next Sunday's bulletin on her computer, he hesitated. Smiling at the middle-aged blonde, he dropped the reports he'd signed into her in-box on the corner of her small desk.

"Can you see that these get mailed to headquarters?" He twisted his wrist to look at his watch, confirming that the time was the same as the clock in his office. "I'm going to be late for my meeting with the contractors."

Sherry Anne picked up the papers and checked the address. "Sure thing. Jacob and Marlene called about their counseling appointment. They want to change it to next week."

"Fit them in." Looking again at his watch, he muttered, "I'm going to be out the rest of the day. Lock up when you leave."

"Sure thing, Pastor." Sherry Anne turned back to her computer screen. "Don't forget your 9:00 a.m. meeting tomorrow with Mr. Bennett. He wants to talk to you about the finances."

Dakota groaned. "Thanks." Zachary Bennett and his wife, Georgia, were huge contributors to the church— and somehow they felt that gave them the right to tell Dakota how to spend church money.

He headed through the foyer. The dark red carpet muffled his footsteps as he passed between the two long middle rows of white pews. The padded seats matched the red of the carpet.

How many times had he looked out over the congregation who filled these pews three times each week? He mentally calculated as he hastened toward the back door and to his appointment. Seven years, nearly three services every week…too many to count.

He continued down the aisle, hearing the air-conditioning turn on. Pausing by the thermostat, he clicked the switch to off. The band had forgotten to turn it off after practice earlier. He made a mental note to mention it to them.

Life was too short, he thought, making a list of things he needed to do. He never had enough hours in the day to get things done. The church currently had no associate pastor, so Dakota was trying to complete all of the pastoral jobs himself. Except for the youth. They did have a great youth pastor—who was still in his office working right now, as a matter of fact.

Working.

Just like Dakota was working, even though he was leaving the church. Just like he'd be working late into the night on a load of reports he'd stashed in his car earlier.

Heading out to his little compact sedan, Dakota tried to think of a time since returning from seminary that he hadn't been busy working on one project or another. There weren't many times, lately. At least he was busy doing God's work, he thought as he pulled out his keys to unlock the door.

But that didn't leave him time for anything else.

Glancing at his watch again, he noted he was going to be late-late-late. He pulled out his cell phone as he unlocked the car, and struggled to balance the phone against his shoulder.

"Call, Chandler Contracts," he spoke into the phone.

The sun was shining brightly today, even though it wasn't hot. Summer was past and fall had finally arrived. The wind whipped at his hair as he finally managed to get the lock turned in the door. Ah, the wind. There was nary a day without it on the plains of Texas.

The phone on the other end began to ring.

He slid into the silver Honda and slipped on the gray seat belt.

He loved his hometown and all that went with it; the weather was great, he knew everyone, it was small enough to get anywhere pretty fast, but it was still big enough to have most of the stores and businesses he might need—like the contractors he was about to hire.

"Chandler Contractors. How may I direct your call?" The deep baritone voice came across the line clearly.

Dakota started his car. "This is Dakota Ryder. I have an appointment with Harry Chandler regarding an extension to our church. I'm running about ten minutes behind. I need you to let him know."

He could hear typing in the background and then, "Very well. Thank you for letting us know, Pastor Ryder."

He shook his head with a slight smile, realizing the young man on the other end of the phone must know him. "No problem."

Clicking the phone off, he dropped it in the empty seat next to him and then pushed the gearshift into Reverse with one hand while twisting the wheel of the car with the other.

Glancing over his shoulder as he backed out, he shook his head. Life couldn't get any more hectic.

Chase Sandoval paused as he set the porcelain figurine over the hearth of the fireplace.

They'd been back barely a week in Shenandoah, Texas, and he had finally started unpacking things beyond the basics they'd needed to survive.

This was why.

The porcelain figure was of a woman wearing a long dress. Her long, wavy hair was pulled back with a blue bow. On her lap sat a tiny child, and the mother stared down lovingly at the child, her arms protecting it carefully.

He'd gotten the figurine for Ruthie when she'd found out she was pregnant with their child.

With Sarah.

Sarah was eleven and his precious Ruthie was gone.

Chase's heart contracted and his hands shook.

Cancer.

Chase and Sarah had watched Ruthie fade away before dying.

Why hadn't she gone for checkups more often? Why had she ignored the signs? More important, why hadn't she told them about her secret?

Angry at first, Chase had finally sunk into acceptance. However, as acceptance had come he'd realized their house in Fort Worth was too empty without her. His job, which had kept him gone so much, now hindered his ability to raise his daughter.

If he'd been around more, perhaps he would have noticed the changes in his wife before it was too late.

But he hadn't and his wife was dead and his daughter was on the road to becoming a juvenile delinquent. She didn't want to be around him or talk to him. She'd started hanging out with some of the bad kids and running the streets. He'd had to find some way to head it off, and quick.

But how?

The house was too empty, his job hours were too long, and his daughter was acting more like eighteen than eleven...

How he had wished he could capture his own childhood and share it with her.

And that's when the idea had struck him.

It'd only taken a few weeks to get a reply back from the local sheriff's office about jobs and then a few more weeks to sell their house.

Then, he'd come back home, to Shenandoah. This was a place where he could raise his daughter, a place to help her find good influences for her life, a place to start over and try to do things right this time. It was a place where they could heal.

Without Ruthie.

Chase hugged the figurine to his chest, and then, with a sigh, reluctantly released his grip on the tiny porcelain figure as he tried to release past pain, setting it upon the hearth just as he tried to set aside the grief and leave it in the past.

The oak hearth was beautifully crafted, the intricate designs made by loving hands. A mirror stretched above the length of the hearth, reflecting Chase's own short, dark brown hair and deep brown eyes. He looked a bit haggard—he needed to step a bit closer to the razor that morning.

He turned his gaze from the mirror, glancing around the room. The floors and ceiling beams were also made of wood and shone as if freshly oiled. The walls were white and the windows were tall and narrow, covered by curtains left by the last owners, who'd said they fit these windows and wouldn't go with their new house.

He appreciated their generous gift.

Still, at moments like this, Chase wondered why he'd bothered with such an elaborate house. There was no one here to care for it, no wife to see that those curtains found matches in furniture or knickknacks.

But he knew.

It was because of Sarah that he'd bought the house.

She needed a home in a good neighborhood with good schools.

The people who had lived here before him had built a fort out back and had a permanent swing set made of wood cemented into the ground. There was a great climbing tree with a picnic table under it. All were constructed with good craftsmanship. He should know—in his spare time he used to build things. He'd gotten some experience here in Shenandoah, working for a carpenter. He loved building and thought Sarah would love the sturdy, beautifully crafted equipment out back, as well as the large spacious room and the quiet small-town feel of Shenandoah.

It would be a place for Sarah.

Staring at the beautiful, though painful, reminder of his beloved wife, Sarah's mother, he decided he'd done enough unpacking for the day. He was going into town for lunch.

He and Sarah could unpack together later. Maybe they'd order a pizza tonight and pop in a movie.

But being in this house, alone, with all of the memories—

Turning away, he headed to the door, scooping up his keys on the way, and leaving the pain for later.

Carolyne Ryder sat in the old-fashioned, padded rocking chair, holding her four-month-old grandson, Joshua. He'd been fussy and unable to go to sleep, while his twin sister, Julie, was resting like a little angel in the crib across the room.

Joshua was asleep now, but Carolyne continued to rock back and forth, back and forth, patting the child's back.

Her daughter, Susan, didn't really need her here. She'd come to that conclusion about three weeks ago. She had a live-in housekeeper who doubled as a nanny and who was there to take care of the kids. Cokie did a great job.

Still, Susan and her husband, Johnny, had insisted that Carolyne stay as long as she wanted. These were her first grandchildren, Susan had only returned to work six weeks ago, and the kids needed a grandmother there for a while longer...

So Carolyne had stayed.

But she was restless. Montana was getting cold, a cold Carolyne wasn't used to, and this just wasn't her home.

Looking around the peach-and-green pastel-shaded room, she smiled at how it had been decorated. Two beautifully multicolored mobiles, one hanging over each crib, danced quietly to their own simple tune, courtesy of the air vent above them that blew out a warm breeze. The cribs had pink-and-blue sheets and baby-bumper pads that were decorated with flounces and tiny teddy bears. A changing table complete with diapers sat between the two cribs.

Carolyne and her husband hadn't had enough money to have anything this fancy when they had been young and Susan had come along. Even when Dakota arrived, they'd been happy just to make ends meet.

Oh, how holding this child brought back such memories of when her own two children were small—and she was needed.

She stared down at the chubby-cheeked, dark-haired baby in her arms.

Now her children were grown. Susan lived half a continent away from Shenandoah and Carolyne's life there, she and Johnny having started their own life with their own friends and their own traditions right here in Montana.

Yes, Susan had her husband and babies, and Carolyne, though she knew would always be welcomed, was no longer needed here.

Susan and Johnny needed time alone. Carolyne might have helped at first, but now she was in the way.

She felt in the way with her son, Dakota, as well. He was the pastor of a growing church that took up most of his time, and he didn't need her anymore, either.

Her husband had died ten years ago, and Carolyne found herself at loose ends. Dakota was so busy with the church that she rarely saw him. He did, however, still live at home with her. She cooked meals, but many days he was so caught up in church work that he missed the meals completely.

She loved him, but she still felt very alone.

Both of her kids were adults.

What was supposed to happen when her kids grew up? What did she have left to look forward to? A simple life, spent growing old in the same house she'd lived in for the last thirty-five years? Would her obituary read that she was fond of puttering in the garden, or that her flower beds took up all of her time? Would her friends say that, yes, she was the one waiting each day for her son to eventually come home and regale her with tales of what went on in his life?

She sighed.

In the other room she heard the phone ring.

Moments later, Cokie entered the room where Carolyne sat, baby in her arms.

Cokie was of Asian descent and one of the nicest women Carolyne had met in Montana. Cokie was quiet. She didn't talk much except to the children. She stayed busy cleaning, cooking or being there for the babies when Carolyne wasn't.

"You have call, Ms. Carolyne." Her softly accented voice drifted quietly to Carolyne.

Surprised, Carolyne wondered who it could be. "Thank you."

She stood and carefully tiptoed over to the crib and laid her grandson down.

She lovingly tucked the small receiving blanket around him and held her breath as he screwed up his mouth. But his eyes remained closed as he adjusted. As he let out a shuddering breath, his tiny fists relaxed next to his head.

Certain he wasn't going to wake up, she left the room and treaded down the light brown carpet into the large living room.

Johnny was a lawyer and evidently did well at his job. The house was beautiful, much bigger than the one Susan had grown up in. With soft earth-toned furniture and brass tables, the living room had a very modern look.

Pity her grandchildren learning to walk in this room, she thought, looking at the many hard surfaces they'd have to crash into as they discovered their balance.

She picked up the phone. "Hello?"

"Carolyne? Is that you?"

"Margaret?" Why in the world would her next-door neighbor be calling her? Color drained from her face as she realized something had happened to Dakota. "Dakota? Is he okay?" Fear clutched her heart.

"Oh, he's fine, he's fine—shush, sister, I'm getting to it," the woman on the line told someone in the background.

Margaret and Mary, twin sisters who had lived next door since Carolyne and her husband had moved in thirty-five years ago, well over eighty now, still bickered as they did when their parents were alive and living in the house with them. "Getting to what? Margaret?" Carolyne asked patiently of the one on the phone. Sometimes she had to prompt the sisters because the two would get so caught up in their own conversation they'd forget who they were actually talking to.

"It's not much, dear," Margaret said now, and Carolyne didn't believe her for a minute. She wouldn't have called if it wasn't much…

"But," Margaret continued, "we wanted you to know we've missed you and so has Dakota. Has he called you much?"

Carolyne took a slow breath and held it for a moment. The two women were up to something. She could sense it. They weren't going to tell her immediately, however. She'd just have to wait them out.

Seating herself in the chair next to the Princess-style phone, she crossed her legs. "No, not today. It's been about a week now since we've talked."

"I thought as much."

"He's a busy man," Carolyne defended her son.

"Is he ever. No, sister, she said he was busy. *Busy.* Now just wait until I'm off the phone. Carolyne, are you still there?"

Carolyne nodded. "Yes, Margaret. As I said, Dakota has his own life. He doesn't need me there or calling him constantly."

"I'm not so sure about that."

Margaret dropped that last sentence and utter silence filled the phone line.

Now they were getting somewhere. But what was this all about? "Why do you say that, Margaret?"

"Well, I'm not one to tell tales, now. You know that, Carolyne dear, but then, when I feel something isn't right, I'm not one to go hide, either. I'm not some faint-hearted girl who simply swoons every time I see something like, well, you know…"

No, she didn't know.

"So, I'm glad it was me that saw it. Yes, sister, and you, too. She always thinks I'm trying to best her, Carolyne. Anyway, *we* saw it. And I felt it my duty to call you."

Margaret took a deep breath, but before she could continue, Mary's voice came across the line. "There's a strange woman on his front doorstep."

"Mary. Get off that extension and let me handle this!"

Carolyne held the phone away from her ear, frowning. Margaret was usually the more practical of the two. What was going on?

"You aren't telling her about the shenanigans, sister, so don't you tell me to get off the phone."

"If you would give me a minute."

Carolyne sighed. Confused, but determined to wade

through their chatter to find out just what was going on, she raised her voice firmly, "What woman?"

"I don't think she's addled or slow, mind you," Margaret butted in over Mary. "To be honest, I don't recognize her at all and I'm sure that Dakota won't either. Anyway, we're about to go over and talk to her."

"We thought about reporting her to the police—" Mary added.

"She's drinking." This from Margaret who attempted to cut Mary's words off.

"And she's dressed, well…indecently," Mary added, not to be outdone.

"Black boots up to her thighs," Margaret supplied.

Alarmed, Carolyne sat up straight, both feet coming to rest on the floor. "Boots to her thighs?"

"And what she's wearing would make anyone blush," Mary said outrageously.

Alarmed, Carolyne tried to tell herself not to over-react. "I'm sure there's some explanation…"

"There sure is," Margaret said bluntly. "Your son needs you. He's not eating supper at home and not getting home until late at night. He's gotten to where it's as late as midnight or more before he makes it home and now this woman is on his doorstep. He's ruining his reputation!"

"Well now, sister," Mary interrupted, "I wouldn't say he's ruining his reputation, but it is obvious that he needs Carolyne back home."

"It's scandalous," Margaret sounded knowing.

"Maybe I should call him," Carolyne's mind whirled in a tizzy over the conversation these two women were attempting to have with her.

"He's not home yet. Believe me, if he was, I'm sure

that woman wouldn't be lolling out on the front porch like she is."

Mary added, "If you were here, everything would be fine. It seems like as soon as you left, Dakota went wild."

"He always was the wilder of the two," Margaret butted in to say.

"I have to agree with sister on that. But I think this is all some mistake. Dakota is a fine man. Still, he has no one here and I think he's lonely."

"Lonely?" Margaret scoffed. "He's so busy he doesn't know what lonely is. Carolyne, we tried calling Pastor Cody at the church and he wasn't there. He's making an early day of it, which means he'll be home soon. If you want my advice, I'd suggest you get home as soon as possible. I think your son needs you."

Carolyne's mind raced.

Dakota didn't need her at all. He was a grown man. Just as her daughter, Susan, was a grown woman.

But hadn't she just been thinking about returning home?

She missed Texas and it was getting too cold here.

She missed her church and the familiar sounds and ease of her own house.

Of course, Dakota didn't really need her, but would it hurt to go ahead and return home early?

"Carolyne, did you hear me?"

"Yes, Margaret, I did. Let me call the airlines, talk to my daughter and see what I can get done, all right?"

"Oh good," Mary said breathlessly. "I'm so glad you're coming back. We've missed sitting out on the porch with you in the evenings."

"Never you mind that, sister," Margaret admonished.

"Her son is under attack and she needs to be here to restore his reputation. Now, get off the phone so I can hang up. Carolyne needs to make plans."

Carolyne heard a click and then Margaret added, "We'll be watching for you."

"I need to make plans first," Carolyne argued.

"No, Carolyne. You need to be here for your son," Margaret's uncharacteristically soft voice touched Carolyne. "Please, hurry home."

Carolyne heard a click and shook her head.

She hung up the phone and then sat staring at it, unsure what was going on at her house. Dakota had been so busy that he rarely had time to call; and when he did, his reports were always filled with what he had to do the next day.

She hadn't pushed talking about how he was doing because he was just so busy.

Maybe she should have.

Could he know the woman who was lounging on their front steps?

Surely not.

If the sisters had described the woman right…unless she was one of Dakota's charity cases, he wouldn't have anything to do with that type of female. Would he?

"Is everything all right, ma'am?"

For the first time, Carolyne noticed Cokie standing there next to her.

"I'm not sure, Cokie. But it looks like I need to go home and find out."

"Ma'am?" Cokie asked.

"I need help packing. It sounds like my son needs me."

Carolyne stood.

Cokie hurried off down the hall and Carolyne picked up the phone to call Susan at work, deciding to call Susan first.

If she planned it right, she could be back home in Texas by dinner.

Dakota Ryder sat in the seat next to his friend, Chase Sandoval. "I appreciate the ride home, Chase. Seems my car won't be ready until tomorrow."

"No problem, bud," Chase replied, his familiar brown eyes glancing toward Dakota as he turned down the tree-lined street. "I can't believe you still live out in this area, man. I remember the years we spent picking leaves up every fall, swearing when we grew up we were going to move where there were no trees." He shook his head. "So, are you gonna hire someone to rake up all the leaves in your yard this fall?"

"You think it's that bad?" Dakota chuckled.

"We spent too many years out there doing it to be forced into doing it anymore."

Dakota laughed outright remembering their childhood adventures together.

"Maybe I'll hire some kids from church. They're getting ready for a winter trip they're planning to take Christmas break, and Jeff has them offering to do jobs for everyone so they can earn money for their expenses."

"Sounds like that new youth pastor of yours is working out."

"He's doing great. A year ago I couldn't have imagined having this many young people attending church."

"Ah, but when you step out on faith and do what God tells you to do…"

Dakota grinned and knew his own brown eyes reflected the humor of Chase quoting back what he'd told him so many times. "It's *my* job to say that." It sure was good to have his old friend back in town. "Yeah, we don't know what God has planned for our future. The church has doubled in size, and we're even looking into doing something special for families around town this Christmas."

Chase turned onto Chippewa where Dakota lived. Dakota tried to look at his neighborhood from his friend's point of view. It was an older area of Shenandoah, a town that wasn't much younger than Fort Worth itself. The streets were laid out in straight lines from north to south and from east to west. Sidewalks graced each side of the street and huge old maple and elm trees filled the front yards. Leaves covered everything, including the streets. The breeze caught a few and they swirled up, dancing across the road in a flurry of movement and color, looking like one of the small twisters that so often invaded their land in the springtime.

The houses themselves were tall and square, mostly made of brick or whitewash, but smaller than the houses in the center of town, and not on such evenly divided lots. By the time a person reached the edge of town, it seemed like wilderness—nothing for miles except the many cattle ranches and a few farmers who grew wheat or cotton.

Dakota had grown up in the house he lived in now. A two-story whitewash, it had a front porch and a swing. Two huge maples stood in the front and a weeping willow and a vegetable garden graced the backyard. The garden had always been his mom's favorite; she loved digging in it, but right now, as autumn deepened its hold, the garden was barren.

"Speaking of the church, it's actually doing very well," Dakota returned to the conversation. "With you back in town you might consider coming there if you don't find another church."

Chase hesitated. "Let me get moved in first."

Because his car had broken down, Dakota had been forced to break his luncheon appointment. But as luck would have it, he'd seen Chase and they'd ended up having lunch together.

His friend wasn't the joking, laughing person he'd remembered. His letters hadn't revealed just how much Chase had suffered since his wife's death. Dakota wondered if he'd backed off from God spiritually as well.

"Shenandoah sure has grown since I've been gone."

Dakota nodded. "I guess twenty years ago everyone thought moving to Fort Worth was the way to go. Now everyone's escaping back out to the small towns within a few hours of the big cities."

"Too much corruption and pollution in the big cities."

"Just why did you move back, Chase?"

Chase had been one of Dakota's best friends growing up. In tenth grade he'd had to move away, but they'd kept in touch over the years through regular mail and e-mail. Last year Chase's wife had died, and Chase had been left to raise their daughter alone.

"You mean besides the job as deputy sheriff?"

Dakota nodded as Chase pulled up at his house. "It looks just the same...except for the two old ladies standing in your yard." Chase nodded toward the house.

Dakota followed his gesture and groaned.

Chase grinned. "What's up with them?"

"That's the Mulgrew sisters. Mary and Margaret. They live next door. Don't you remember them?"

Chase's eyes widened. "Wait a minute...you mean they're still alive?"

Dakota nodded. "Alive and well and out to take care of me now that my mom is visiting Susan and helping take care of the twins."

Chase unsnapped his seat belt and jumped from the sedan. Dakota followed suit. Reaching into the back of the car, he grabbed one of the two boxes he'd put in his car, intending to bring them home before his transmission had given out.

"I'll help you with those," Chase offered.

"You just want to see what the Mulgrew sisters have to say."

Chase chuckled, the first real laugh he'd heard from his friend since meeting up with him again. "They were a pair back then."

They started up the leaf-covered sidewalk toward the house. Mary and Margaret both wasted no time in hurrying toward them.

The shorter of the two, Mary, her light blue hair distinguishing her from her older (by only a few minutes) sister, who had silver hair, started forward. "It's awful. I told her she shouldn't be up there, but she just laughed in my face, didn't she, sister?"

Margaret nodded. "And rather rudely. She's had a

nip." Margaret motioned with her hand, as if tipping a bottle up, and then dropped it into her other hand, clasping them, worrying the white hankie that was in her other hand. "Bless your mother's heart. If she saw that she'd turn white with shock."

"Not sister and me though," Mary added. "I do say, it is shocking, but then, we grew up in poverty and saw worse back then, though you didn't flaunt it."

"Well, you did if you were one of them," Margaret lifted an eyebrow to match her superior tone.

"Margaret," Mary admonished.

Dakota raised a hand. "Um, excuse me."

Both women turned from each other to look at him expectantly. Before he could say a word, however, Margaret launched back into her speech. "We thought about calling the police but then, you are a pastor and are supposed to have mercy and we decided you'd probably seek out a homeless shelter—"

"Or something," Mary added, not to be left out.

"I'm not sure…that is…" Dakota began trying to decide what to address first in all they had just said. These women had a way of turning his dark brown hair a bit grayer with every meeting. He was certain those first few gray hairs he'd found the other day were attributable to conversations like this.

"Have we met?" Margaret interrupted, staring oddly at Chase. "You look familiar."

Chase cleared his throat. "I'm Chase Sandoval, ma'am."

"Oh, yes!" Mary nodded suddenly. "You were that boy that liked to ride his bike through our yard."

Chase actually blushed to the roots of his hair. "Oh,

yeah, I'd, um…forgotten." He cast a look at Dakota, hoping for help.

Dakota was still trying to figure out why he'd want to contact a homeless shelter.

"We certainly didn't forget," Margaret told him. "I always worried you were going to grow up to be a hoodlum. Looks like you turned out good—unless you're here for counseling from Pastor Cody."

"Pastor—"

"Cody…" Dakota acknowledged. "They're the only ones who still call me that name." He smiled patiently. "But he's not. Here for counseling, that is. Which brings us around full court. Can you tell me, ladies, why I might want to call a homeless shelter?"

The sound of his swing creaking brought his head around to his porch—and his jaw dropped.

A woman, no more than five and a half feet tall, stood up. It wasn't just a woman though, it was…he glanced at her outfit and saw why Margaret and Mary had worried about who was on his porch.

Moving past the two women, he headed toward the steps and slowly climbed to the porch. *Father, guide me,* he prayed silently, wondering how this woman had found his address.

Her black skirt hung at an odd angle and stopped just above her knees—it might have once been a possible accessory to a business suit. However, one boot was missing a heel, and her sweater hung off one shoulder, nearly exposing areas that Dakota had no business seeing. Her hair was ratted, big enough a bird's nest could hide in it, and the smeared and caked-on makeup on her face easily added a pound to her weight—her very light weight. Her high cheekbones were gaunt, and her bleary eyes stared out at him from under mascara-smeared lids.

He didn't miss the bottle of booze in her hand. Nor could he miss the smell. "Hello, I'm Dakota Ryder. Can I help you?"

Compassion filled him at the empty look in her eyes. Compassion and concern as she teetered on her feet. Taking a step forward, she waved the bottle. "How ya doing, Cody? We said we'd be best friends forever." She giggled and took another swig of the bottle before tossing it over the porch rail and into the flower bed. "I'm here to be your sister." With that, she threw out her arms, promptly lost her balance and fell headlong into the stunned arms of Dakota Ryder.

Chapter Two

"Whoa, Dakota!"

Chase came rushing up the stairs, dropping the box he'd been carrying, intending to help his friend.

Dakota lay, stunned, beneath an unconscious body that smelled like the sewers of Fort Worth, boxes scattered about him. Shifting, he managed to get to his knees and then lifted the woman into his arms. With Chase's help, he stood. Then, fumbling in his pocket, he managed to find and toss his keys to Chase. "Will you get the door?"

"Sure thing."

"Can we help?"

Margaret and Mary were both standing at the foot of the stairs.

Not sure what to say, he hesitated before finally nodding. "She's gonna need some hot coffee and soup, if you wouldn't mind." The two women were eccentric but loved to help, and he knew they'd appreciate having something to do. Especially when they'd be able to tell the entire town, for months to come, how they'd gotten to assist the pastor in taking care of her

Chase pulled the screen door open and then shoved the large oak door inward.

Dakota strode in, carefully carrying his bundle into his childhood home. His feet echoed hollowly on the old wooden floor as he crossed the foyer before stepping onto the rug near the sofa. Shoving two of the decorative pillows out of the way, he deposited his load on the brocade couch.

She was definitely out. Leaning forward to examine her, he held his breath. The fumes alone were enough to make him drunk. *Dear God, who is she and why is she here?* he prayed silently. Checking her pulse, he found it strong and steady. At least that was a good thing.

"I'll get the boxes," Chase murmured and left the house.

Dakota made a call to a friend who was a doctor, asking him to come by, and then he went to his closet to get a blanket. Actually, the less Mary and Margaret saw of the woman, the better. The less any of them saw, the better, he thought.

Bending down, he patted the woman's cheek.

The screen door squeaked as Chase came back inside. "Your box is a bit banged up but it looks okay. Hope you don't have anything breakable in it or the other one."

Dakota blinked. His eyes watered at the smell the woman exuded. Going to a window, he shoved first one and then another open. "No. They were just papers and other things I had to go over. It's getting close to the end of the year and we're thinking of changing a lot of the church curriculum. We are also going over the mission budget and I wanted to review everything personally." He shook his head at the smell as it filled his nostrils.

Chase sidled over toward the window. "No one can say life as a pastor isn't interesting. Tell me, do you know her?"

Dakota started to shake his head then paused. "She said she was here to be my sister," he murmured.

"That's not sister's garb she's wearing," Chase mocked.

Dakota shot him a look. "The words rang a bell. I just can't place them."

Taking a deep breath, he steeled himself before moving back to her side. "It's possible someone sent her to me for help. It certainly wouldn't be the first time, though I think she managed to shock my neighbors, which is a first."

"They remembered my bike," Chase muttered.

Dakota finally grinned. "They don't forget much."

"You don't say? That was over twenty years ago."

Dakota nodded. "You should try living next door to them. Anytime I think of getting a big head over something, they remind me of things that promptly knock it back down. They're also on the lookout for a woman for me."

Chase shook his head, grinning.

"Yeah, and they used to question each girl I brought home for Mom to meet. Only after Dad died, that is."

Dakota's dad had died in a granary explosion ten years earlier, leaving his mom and her children dependent on each other. Dakota had done his best by working odd jobs to help take care of bills, hating to see his mom working in a nursing home cafeteria for a living. "The sisters were also a blessing during that time after Dad died," he added, remembering. "Anyway, it's been an adventure with them as neighbors."

Silence fell.

Chase shifted on his feet, slipping both hands into his front pockets. His wavy dark hair hung forward over one eyebrow as he bounced on his heels. "So, have you figured out who she is yet?"

Dakota looked back at her. Very light skin and blond hair, whether it was real or not he wasn't sure. The woman had a nice figure, not overblown but just right except she was a bit underweight. He would bet she'd clean up pretty and would probably be a knockout. Right now though, with her makeup smeared, black eyeliner making her look as if she had twin black eyes, he doubted her own mother could identify her. "Nope. I don't know who she is. But it's obvious she knows me." The smell was actually subsiding, or maybe he was just getting used to it, but he realized it wasn't bothering him as much now as it had a moment ago.

A knock on the door interrupted them. Mary and Margaret each carried a pot in their hands.

"That was certainly fast," Chase murmured.

Dakota crossed to the door. "Come in, ladies."

"Oh, we can't stay," Mary's blue hair was bobbing as she came inside. "But here's the coffee."

"And here's some soup left over from what we had yesterday. We had thought to bring it over to you today if you wanted it. So, it ended up here anyway." Margaret gave him a warm smile.

Dakota took the time to return her smile and take the coffeepot from Mary. He crossed the wooden floor past the sofa into the dining room. Grabbing a hot pad from the side table, he placed it on the large round wooden table and then set down his load.

He turned and saw Margaret had followed him, so he did the same with the soup bowl.

"No hurry in getting these dishes back. You just take care of that woman on your sofa."

Dakota glanced behind him at the door to the kitchen and thought about getting cups and bowls but decided that could wait. "Thank you, ma'am," he murmured.

"She looks so bad."

Dakota turned to see Mary standing near Chase, wringing her hands, staring at the woman on the sofa.

"When she wakes up you should make sure she bathes. But not here. That wouldn't be proper. You'll have to find somewhere else for her to clean up."

"I'm sure we'll think of something," Dakota reassured Mary.

"You don't want your mama's reputation ruined, or yours, Pastor. Think about that," Margaret informed him.

He nodded. "I will."

Margaret reached out and patted his arm. "We should go, Mary, so the pastor can get about his work of converting this woman."

Dakota saw Chase cover a smile with his hand. "Thank you both." Dakota strode back through the living room to the screen door. "I'm sure the woman will appreciate the food—once she's awake. You've saved me a heavy chore of having to cook."

Both ladies beamed at the compliment. Mary actually giggled like a schoolgirl. "If you need anything else," Mary called as they toddled out onto the wooden porch.

"I'll be sure to call," he affirmed.

Once they were safely down the stairs, Dakota let the screen door close.

Chase chuckled.

"They're concerned," Dakota informed him.

"I noticed." Glancing around, he noted, "The place sure hasn't changed much since we were kids."

"You don't think so?"

Dakota glanced around too, trying to see it through the eyes of his childhood. The old braided rug he'd grown up with continued to grace the middle of the room with the old-fashioned sofa and coffee table sitting on one edge. The brocaded chairs and love seat each had their own braided rugs. The fireplace still had family pictures on it. Both of the tall front windows had lace curtains just like when he was a child, but he had added miniblinds to them about five years ago.

The pictures on the walls had once been of oceans but his mom had talked so much about the prairie that for a Christmas present about four years ago, he'd bought her three new pictures. One was of a wooden fence and a windmill at sunset with only the flat plain behind it. The second was of an old ranch house and a horse grazing in the front yard. The third was the picture of a Native American on a horse, both drooping wearily.

The dining room had not changed, with the same side table and dining table as well as the cupboard. The dishes were the only thing different. In the kitchen, however, there were all new appliances.

Suddenly he realized that despite the changes he'd made, the house was still basically the same. "I guess I don't see much reason to alter things," Dakota murmured.

"Which is why you're still here in town when many of us left and made the few hours' bus ride to Fort Worth."

Dakota admitted he was right. He liked things to stay the same. He'd slipped easily into the role of pastor in town after he'd gotten back from his training. The entire time he'd been gone had seemed to be a waste. Now he wondered if that emotion hadn't simply been his desire to be back home.

"So, what are you going to do about her?" Chase motioned toward the woman on the sofa.

She shifted onto her side, moving to get comfortable but not waking up.

"I guess we'll wait until the doctor gets here and then decide."

Chase nodded. "I should go. My mother-in-law is with Sarah and I promised to get back. She's headed back to Dallas tomorrow."

Dakota wasn't sure what to say, not wanting to be left alone with a woman in his house. He was saved by the doctor pulling up outside. With a silent prayer of thanks, Dakota nodded. "It was great seeing you again, Chase. I'm only sorry our day turned out this way."

"Hey, bud." Chase shrugged. "How could you know this was going to happen?"

Dakota walked to the door and pulled it open.

"Call me if you need anything else." With a look at

the woman on the sofa, Chase headed out and down the stairs just as Dr. Joshua Meadows climbed them.

"So, what's this about an inebriated woman, Dakota?"

Dakota stepped back and motioned to the sofa. "She was on my doorstep when I got home, Josh. I really would appreciate it if you'd examine her and make sure she's okay. Frankly, I'm not sure what to do with her."

Josh lifted an eyebrow and grinned. With dark brown hair and a sense of humor, Josh was a good doctor. Tall and athletic, he enjoyed basketball and lifting weights. Dakota sometimes worked out with him. "Well, let's do one thing at a time. Can you call Mary and have her come over here to witness while I examine the woman?"

Dakota felt relief now that Josh was here. They'd been friends since Dakota had first taken over pastoring Shenandoah Family Church. When he'd been unsure about pastoring the same people he'd grown up with, Josh, new in town, had been a friend he could confide in. Their paths often crossed in professional ways, which had helped develop their friendship.

Law wasn't something Dakota thought about much, but it was something Josh did consider. And Dakota was glad. He didn't like to think about how it might be with him alone in the house. The brown eyes of the doctor, however, were sharp and full of implication.

Going to the phone, he called Mary and asked her if she'd mind helping the doctor. Then he returned to Josh's side.

"What can you tell me about her?" Josh asked now, setting down his black bag and pulling out a stethoscope and blood pressure cuff.

"I came home. She had a bottle of whiskey in her hands. She took a drink, tossed the bottle, stumbled and passed out."

Josh nodded. "And you don't want to call the police…"

"She hasn't done anything. If she's come to me for help—which I think she has—then jail isn't the place for her. I can't send her to a homeless shelter like this. The closest shelter is about two hours away! But I can't toss her out."

As Dakota explained the situation, his own situation became clear. He couldn't very well keep the woman here. He didn't know anything about her. But he couldn't put her out either.

But he could *not* keep her here.

Oh boy, he thought dismally, not sure what he was going to do.

Mary arrived. He went to the door and let her in just as the phone rang. Crossing the living room to the table next to the love seat, he answered, leaving Josh and Mary to the patient. "Hello?"

"Dakota honey?"

How did she always know? Dakota wondered. "Hi, Mom. What's up?"

"I have good news. I'm booked on a flight back to Shenandoah at 5:00 p.m. tonight and wondered if you would be able to pick me up at the airport." His mom's voice was so matter-of-fact—as if it was normal for her to call unexpectedly when his life was suddenly upside down, only to announce she was coming home.

"I thought you were planning on staying at least another month to help Susan with the twins." Suspicious, he fished for something to tell him what his mother knew. Small towns, he thought, almost certain someone had called her about the woman on his steps.

"I've been here three months already, honey." That much was true.

Glancing over to the sofa, he saw Mary, hands clasped, looking overly innocent and wide eyed as she stared at him.

He had his answer.

"I see."

"I'm sure you do," his mother said wisely.

"I'll be glad to make sure someone is there to pick you up at the airport, Mom. However, I have company, so I won't be able to make it myself."

He waited for a response. A question. Something. When it came, it was simple. "That's fine. See you around five-thirty. Bye, son."

"Goodbye, Mom."

He hung up the phone.

"Who was that?"

Dakota turned to Mary and gave her one of his you've-been-meddling-again looks. Then he turned to Josh. "That was Mom. She's on her way home."

"Word travels fast."

"Uh-huh." He shot a look at Mary, who would have been whistling if she knew how. In all the years he'd known her, he knew that whistling had been a bone of contention between the two sisters. Margaret could whistle. Mary could not.

"What about our patient?" he asked, changing the subject. It wouldn't do any good to get onto Mary for calling his mom. She watched out for him whether he wanted it or not. And if she felt his mom would be a help here—which, he had to admit, she would since he couldn't very well throw an unconscious woman out on the street—then Mary and Margaret would call his mom.

Thirty-two years old and they still treated him as if he were twelve.

"Blood pressure is okay. So are her heart and lungs, pupils. I'd say she's going to be fine. She just needs to sleep it off. You won't get any answers out of her today, I'm afraid."

Dakota nodded. "I guess that's that then."

"Want me to put her in the spare room?"

Dakota hesitated.

Mary piped up, "It wouldn't be right for you to be alone here. I'll be glad to stay with you. Besides, you promised me over a month ago to help me with that puzzle I'm working. I'll call Margaret and have her bring it over and we can finish it together."

Great. An afternoon with Margaret and Mary.

But at least the woman would feel safe when she woke and found herself in his house—and he'd feel safe, too, when he faced his congregation.

It seemed the best choice. "That sounds great, Mary."

Josh shifted the woman on the sofa and lifted her. "Lead the way."

Chapter Three

Dark shadows surrounded her and she knew the dream was starting again. No amount of liquor could keep the demons at bay. And as the deep dark recesses parted and the fog swirled away from around her, she knew what was coming. As a spectator in a theater seat, she watched the past play out before her once again.

It started out the same every time. She was falling down the set of stairs, falling, grasping for the handrail. She'd been fine, laughing with her friend, and then had simply missed a step. Or she'd thought that was it.

Shouts sounded and people came running. One of her co-workers helped her up. But she couldn't stand. She must have hurt her leg.

Her boss gave her the rest of the day off.

She went home and took a hot bath.

She'd thought a hot bath would help her pain, ease the aches of the fall, but it hadn't.

Instead of getting better, she found she couldn't get out of the tub.

Panic ensued. But in the dream the water was drowning her, pulling her down below the rim, in the tub, alone, with no help.

The water had eventually chilled and slowly her leg had started working; gradually the water released its death hold on her.

Trembling, she'd pulled herself out of the tub and managed to get to her bed.

Falling onto the soft white sheets, she thought to sleep off the scare. Of course, the dream didn't end. Instead, she saw herself decide to get up and go to work. It was unexplainably day again. Birds were singing. A soft breeze blew in the curtained window.

Mists swirled in around her, trying to block her vision of the deceptively beautiful day. As she was back at work, jokes floated off the tongues of her friends, silly jokes about her being a klutz. Her leg had gotten better and she was back, but this day, not even a month later according to the calendar on her desk, her hand was going numb.

Her boss, Rob, was standing there, waiting on a report, saying it was about time she got some rest, when he noticed she'd stopped typing.

Her arm burned, burned from shoulder to elbow, and her fingers didn't want to work. Flames were leaping from her arm.

Cold crept up her spine, extinguishing the flames, but not before her boss saw them.

He insisted she take the day off and go to the doctor. That was it. He didn't try to put the flames out or comment on them, just told her to go see a physician.

He forced her toward the door, grabbing her arm,

shoving at her. She stepped toward his office and right into the ER.

The three days of testing played like a video on fast-forward. And they were very true to what had really happened.

There was the doctor. Then radiology.

A spinal tap.

There were machines hooked up to her that made her muscles jump and dance. Her arms and legs looked like a caricature of Pinocchio when he danced.

And then she was sitting in the doctor's office, those strings still on her, moving her arms and legs…until he told her the diagnosis.

The verdict.

The strings fell off.

Shock stunned her speechless.

Her grandmother appeared, in her wheelchair next to her, her voice like the teacher's on Charlie Brown, there but indistinguishable. The only sound she could make out was that of her grandmother's anger as she swung a stick at her and then cackled with glee.

It wasn't thought to be hereditary, the doctor had told her—but then he didn't know about her grandmother. He couldn't see her grandmother laughing at her.

Why couldn't he?

She looked from him to her grandmother and back.

They didn't know what caused it.

She felt hysterical laughter bubbling up in her.

He asked her if she was okay then told her they needed to talk about the next steps.

But she knew there was no treatment. Just look at her horrible grandmother!

Her hateful, wheelchair-bound grandmother who loved to hit her with a stick and who taunted and tormented her mother and father until Daddy had left and Mother had finally moved to the city to try to make enough money for them to survive.

What was she going to do?

The scene changed and pictures started moving faster and faster through her mind.

She was at work, but only for a month.

She was trying to type, but crying instead.

She heard the whispers, saw the looks. It wasn't good for business for her to be seen like that.

Just a drink to help get her through the stares, to help her forget what the doctor had told her.

She saw herself hitting the answering machine over and over, erasing messages from the doctor's office.

Why wouldn't they leave her alone?

She couldn't sleep, couldn't eat, couldn't work.

And then Rob had let her go.

Oh, he'd been nice about it. He'd told her if she got her act together, to give him a call. She saw the smile on his face, that fake smile, painted on much like a clown's face.

And she realized she was already changing. She wasn't like she was before. Nice, carefree, fun-loving. No, she was changing into the monster of her past—her grandmother.

She couldn't think about it.

She wouldn't think about it.

Driving home she'd nearly hit a man crossing the street.

That had been the final straw.

With her last paycheck, she walked into a liquor store and bought enough liquor to help her forget.

The mists swirled in and she relaxed, until she heard the pounding and realized the dream wasn't over.

Oh, no, she saw the car being towed and an eviction notice nailed to her door. The scenes swirled madly.

She was on the street.

She tried a homeless shelter, but was almost raped that night and fled.

She'd demanded more liquor, anything to help her not remember, not know where she was.

She didn't want to remember what had been said.

Life wasn't fair.

She'd lost her mom and now this.

She wanted hope again.

But there was no hope here, no life, nothing for her.

In the deepest despair she'd ever been in, she remembered another time of deep despair, of a time she had been forced to lose her best friend.

Yet, in that despair, a line floated into her remembrance.

If you ever need me, I'll be here.

If only that were true, she thought.

She tipped the bottle and drank.

And walked. She watched herself head off down the street, the empty, black, lonely street, the mist parting as she walked.

She didn't go to pay the creditors or to the homeless shelter. She headed toward the one ray of hope in a life suddenly filled with desperation and emptiness.

And then the dream ended and she opened her eyes in a strange house.

And she realized, suddenly, that somehow she'd made her wish come true. At least she was certain she'd somehow found her way back to the past, back to Dakota Ryder's house, and she was lying there now being tucked in to bed by a man with a stethoscope.

His eyes met hers and she stiffened, waiting for the worst. The man smiled gently and whispered, "Go back to sleep."

And that's exactly what Meghan O'Halleran did. She closed her eyes and tried to get back into the dream of the little girl in a soft bed—because she knew what she'd just seen couldn't be reality. Not for her. Not for an O'Halleran.

Safety and love could only come true in her dreams.

Chapter Four

He had thought about her all night. After his mom had arrived home. And the explanations for her presence had been few. She must have missed the bus and someone had sent her his way.

"Good morning, Dakota."

Cody stopped at the sideboard in the dining room to pour himself a cup of coffee. Though his diminutive mother was now gray-haired and her hands had begun to show signs of age, those blue eyes of hers missed nothing. And though she didn't demand questions, that wasn't her style, he knew she was there, waiting to listen. When had she stopped being just a mom and become a friend? Nodding to his mom, he started around the table, pausing to kiss her cheek. So who was the woman who had said she was his "sister"? Cody thought once again as he had a dozen times last night.

"Is our guest up?" he asked as he took his seat across from his mom and picked up the morning paper.

He liked to go through the hospital and death section

to keep up on the residents and what someone might be going through in town. Perhaps there was a hint of the woman upstairs, if someone was missing or such.

"Not yet," his mother murmured. "Are you ready to talk?"

"About what?" he asked, though he knew exactly what his mother wanted to say. He was too busy to encourage her. He had to get to work, see about meeting Chandler's concerning the new wing on the church. The reports he'd brought home still needed to be gone over, among a dozen other things. Of course, he'd known his mom would want to discuss the woman since she hadn't said a word about it yesterday. The problem was, he didn't know anything.

"Your guest."

"My…" He paused and glanced up over the paper then shook his head. "She's not *my guest,* Mother. She is someone who needed a place to stay and since we don't have a shelter in town, I put her up." Her face, slightly rounded though elegant and graceful, wore a soft smile as she waited—and that was more convincing than anything else. "Besides," he added, returning to scanning the paper before taking a sip of the hot black coffee he'd poured himself, "she was unconscious. What was I supposed to do?"

Okay, he felt a bit odd having a drunk in his house— his mother's house. A drunk woman, actually. This was a first. He'd had many men come to his door drunk, he usually just let them sleep in the small apartment over the garage out back, and then in the morning, he showed up with coffee and an ear to listen.

Never had a woman shown up on his doorstep and embraced him as she had—and then promptly passed out.

Yes, this was definitely a first. The reason why *she* was upstairs and not out back like a *guy*. He shook his head again.

"I suppose you should have done whatever you felt you should have done with the guest." His mother went back to sipping her coffee.

He didn't know what to do with the woman, and frankly, he was still a bit uncomfortable over yesterday.

Wearily he set aside the paper. "I really need to get to work."

His mother didn't comment.

Uncomfortable, he asked, "Do you think you can stay here until she wakes up?" He glanced at his watch. "I'm supposed to meet about the construction on the church in an hour."

When his mom didn't answer immediately, he sighed. "I can call an officer to come over. Jerry would be glad to be here with you when she wakes up."

Dakota could tell his mom was disappointed. Frustrated, he wanted to tell her he was busy, so busy that he was meeting himself coming and going. He didn't need one more unexpected thing added to his list—like this woman.

Immediately his spirit stabbed at his conscience. That was his job. Of course, it should be added to his list.

"I'm sorry, Mom. I suppose I can call and reschedule."

Instead of rebuking him, his mom set aside her coffee cup and folded her hands. With understanding, she studied him. "I'll be fine, Dakota. If you have to go, then you have to go. I'll be glad to be here when the woman wakes up." She paused and then added, "Can you tell me her name before you go?"

Her name. If only he knew her name. Of course, if he stayed around, he would get a chance to talk to her and find out. And really, this wasn't his mom's job, but his job. Guiltily, he shook his head. "Like I said last night. She passed out right after I arrived."

His mother's lips twitched slightly. "Mary and Margaret have a different take on it, I'm afraid."

Dakota grimaced. He'd heard the phone ring earlier this morning and had just been certain it was his neighbors. They'd actually left him and his mom in peace last night. He'd expected Mary or Margaret to launch into a lengthy explanation as soon as his mom had arrived home.

Instead, they'd patted her hand and told her that all would be well now that she was there and tottered off home—after they had stayed to finish the puzzle, and regale him with tales of every puzzle they had ever put together. Boy, had last night been a night.

"I can only imagine what they said," Dakota muttered, figuring they would get to it eventually. He'd seen that look the sisters had shared when his mom had sat down to help with the puzzle.

"Dakota!" his mother admonished, even though she was forcing her smile away as she spoke.

"Okay, out with it." Dakota glanced at his watch and decided he had enough time to hear this before he left. If he left. He felt himself wavering as God spoke to his heart.

His mother shook her head. "That she dressed scandalously and embraced you were a couple of their comments."

Dakota groaned. This was going to take more than a few minutes. It always did when it involved those two ladies.

"Just as I thought." His mother chuckled. "Why don't you tell me the entire story?"

"She wasn't dressed scandalously, Mom." He sat back and prepared to tell his side of the story. Lifting his cup to his lips, he took a sip of his coffee while his mom waited. Setting it aside, he leaned back in his chair, crossed his legs, and began, hesitantly, being careful to be honest but not gossipy. "She looked as if she hadn't bathed in a month and her makeup was smeared." He remembered how shocked he'd been at her appearance, how he'd ached wondering what this poor woman had been through. "Her top was askew and one heel on a boot was broken." He forced his inward gaze back to his mom. "I've seen people in similar situations, Mom. Mary and Margaret were simply exaggerating. It was the attack as I came up the porch that threw me, however, and probably what fueled the sisters' imaginations. The woman told me she wanted to be my sister and then she lunged out at me."

He shifted uncomfortably. He loved his mom and cared what she thought, but it was embarrassing to tell her about that bit.

His mom didn't laugh, however. Instead, she frowned. "Your *sister?*"

He nodded. "We're not Catholic and she's not a nun. I would swear her showing up here was simply an accident, but if it is…" He lifted a hand and ran it through his hair in frustration. "What could she have meant?"

His mother rested one hand on top of the other, her brow furrowing as she contemplated what Cody had said. "Maybe your reasoning is where the problem is."

"What?" He resisted the urge to glance at his watch. "How do you mean?"

"Well, she hugs you, calls herself a sister…so perhaps you *do* know her."

Dakota shook his head. "I haven't met her before, Mom. I would remember her."

His mom lifted an eyebrow in a way only a mother can and he squirmed in response. "I meant that she's a grown woman and in my line of work—"

"Maybe she wasn't an adult when you met her. Tell me exactly what she said yesterday."

Dakota felt time slipping away and knew he was going to be late. But, to solve this dilemma he needed to recount the story, find an answer and then see to helping this woman. Chandler's would just have to wait.

Quickly and concisely, he related all she had said.

Slowly, his mom nodded. "Think back to your teenage years. You were always so generous. Is it possible you told someone they could move in with us and she could be your sister?"

Dakota shook his head, then paused. "I wouldn't have told any girl she could be my sister, but…"

His mom cocked her head in sudden thought. "There was a little girl, a long time ago. You might not even remember her." Carolyne paused and studied her son. "She was very special to you. She used to take your side whenever you and your sister would fight."

Dakota's eyes widened. The past came flooding back. Something in grade school he remembered. A playground and a little blond-haired girl. They had spit in each other's hand. It was fuzzy, but he remembered some incident about her leaving and he didn't want to lose her... "Molly, Marsha..."

"Meghan."

"Meghan!" Dakota repeated after his mother and leaned forward, shaking his head in disbelief. He hadn't thought of her in ages. "That's impossible. It's been so many years. I wouldn't know her. She wouldn't know me."

"But you did used to call her your best friend."

"She had blond hair, was skinny." Dakota shook his head, unable to believe what his mom had suggested. "I don't remember much except that she liked to make mud pies and we liked to swing on the swing set."

It couldn't be, he thought. What would she be doing back here? "Last I heard they moved to Fort Worth." He paused and then mused aloud. "I always did wonder what happened to her."

"The young woman is blond," Dakota heard his mom say. "She called herself your best friend. True, she was inebriated at the time, but be that as it may, whether it is or is not Meghan, there is one thing you do know."

"What's that?" Dakota asked as more and more snatches of memories presented themselves about a young girl he'd once known.

"She came to you for help."

Dakota snapped to attention as compassion flooded him. Contrite, he realized his mom had made her point without chiding him once.

He nodded. "Yes, she did."

Guilty that he had been in such a hurry, he admitted how wise his mother was. Wisdom came with years and his mom was one of those who had helped guide him and direct him with sage words of advice. She didn't correct him often, but when she did, she was usually right.

"Excuse me?"

Both mother and son turned at the timid sound.

Dakota had tarried too long, for their guest stood at the bottom of the stairs, dressed in her outfit of the day before and looking much the worse for wear.

He would have known she was there had she not said anything when the smell hit him.

Yet, his compassion only grew as he saw the fear, embarrassment and reserved look in the way she stood, arms crossed across her stomach as if holding herself against any onslaught they might make. Her gaze shifted to his mom and then back to him.

"I am really sorry but…" The woman's voice came out hoarse and she winced, then lifted a hand to her head. Hangover headache, he thought.

"Mrs. Ryder?" she asked, though her gaze was on Dakota. Finally, it turned back to his mother.

His mom rose smoothly and crossed to her. "I am— Carolyne Ryder."

The woman stumbled slightly and righted herself. Her cheeks grew a soft rosy pink though the embarrassment in her eyes reflected self-recrimination.

"I'm so sorry. I should go." She tried to back away, the embarrassment growing. "I don't know how I ended up here—"

"Nonsense." His mother slipped an arm around her to keep her from exiting. She did not once blink over the powerful stench the woman exuded. His mother was full of grace and love—and she always had been.

As they started toward the table, Dakota noticed the woman dragged one leg just a bit and wobbled as she walked. He wondered if she'd hurt herself yesterday when she fell and made a note to call the doctor about it.

"Really," the young woman continued even as his mother firmly led her to the table so she could sit down. "I didn't mean to come here, that is—"

"Would you like some coffee? We've been trying to guess your identity."

The woman's cheeks turned even redder, the color leeching down into her neck.

Dakota couldn't stay quiet any longer. "Meghan?" he asked, needing to know.

The woman stopped dead and then promptly burst into tears.

Aghast, Dakota looked at his mom, who met his gaze over the woman's head.

What had he said?

"There, there," his mother murmured and pulled the girl into her arms.

Dakota didn't know what to do. He prayed a quiet prayer for guidance and allowed himself to slip into his pastoral mode, as he thought of it, caring but detached from the situation.

He observed as his mom held the woman and smoothed her ratty hair, praying quietly for God to comfort the woman and for guidance when she was finally able to talk.

Slowly the woman's tears subsided.

His mom pushed a tissue into her hand and she wiped her eyes, smearing the leftovers of makeup even worse.

Cody didn't mind.

All that was left in his heart now was concern and compassion. It didn't matter how she smelled, how she looked, who she was.

The woman was full of pain and needed someone to talk with.

He saw her dart a glance at him before wiping at her nose and took that as a signal to intervene.

"You are welcome here, Meghan," he said gently and waited.

Meghan shuddered and took a fresh tissue. She wiped at her eyes again and then, after taking a deep breath, she whispered, "I didn't mean to show up here. I—oh dear."

She glanced up at his mom and saw only compassion as Carolyne nodded to her. She straightened her shoulders and pushed away, becoming an isolated tower as she tried to pull dignity about her. "I don't usually drink," she confessed. "Until lately. I was so…inebriated that I guess I didn't realize what I was doing. I thought it was a dream, really. I mean, I came back…"

She trailed off.

Cody steepled his fingers and leaned back, crossing his legs once again. "Why did you come back, Meghan?" he prompted gently when she didn't continue.

She stiffened.

"It's okay, Meghan…" Cody's mother patted her leg, leaving her hand resting there in silent support.

Meghan's eyes, the beautiful green that he could see today, focused on his mom and tension drained. Finally, she confessed, "I didn't know where else to go."

His mom's eyes turned to and rested in his gaze.

Cody knew that look.

And he knew the signs from the woman in front of him. She was exhausted.

"I am so sorry—" Meghan began.

"Mom, is the electricity on in the garage apartment?" Cody cut in, ignoring the woman's protest.

His mom smiled, approval in her eyes.

"I just have to flip the circuit breaker."

"What?" Meghan looked from one to the other.

"You don't have to say anything more, Meghan," Cody told her. "We have a place you can stay."

"Here?" She was genuinely surprised, though he saw sudden hope in her eyes.

Dakota nodded.

"We don't have a shelter in town." His mom smiled. "And besides, we have that apartment back there not being used."

"Oh, I couldn't possibly—" Meghan began.

"Of course you can." His mom patted Meghan's arm. "I'm sure you want to bathe and need time to regroup."

"But I haven't even explained why I'm here," Meghan protested.

Cody could see in her eyes that she wanted to stay, that she didn't want to explain, and that she needed time to regroup.

Her story would come out in time.

"No need to explain." When Meghan looked at him questioningly, he shrugged. "God sent you to us. I imagine He knows why you're here, and if you want to talk later, my mom or I will be willing to listen."

"You don't really know me, though," Meghan whispered.

"We don't have to know you, Meghan. God only tells us to love you."

Fresh tears filled her eyes.

His mom nodded and then turned to Meghan. "Let's go upstairs. I'll see if I can find you some fresh clothes." She had maneuvered Meghan to a standing position and together they turned and started toward the stairs. His mother continued, "We'll run a bath and afterward we'll have some breakfast. I'm sure you'll feel much better by then."

As their voices faded, Cody smiled.

That was his mom.

Indispensable.

She knew the right thing to say and do and wasn't above bullying if the need arose—but in her own gentle way.

He glanced at his watch.

He wouldn't be too late if he left now.

He could meet with Chandler's, get done what he needed to get done and be back after his new guest had time to bathe and gather herself.

Thank you, Father. His prayer was short and simple, then he stood. *Take care of her,* he added and headed for the door, wondering just what tale his guest was going to have to share and wondering just why God had brought her back to Shenandoah and into his life.

Chapter Five

"I can't believe this town hasn't changed in twenty years." Chase walked down the sidewalk next to Jerry Duffy, sheriff of Shenandoah.

Jerry was on the older side, approaching sixty, and he smiled at Chase's comment. "Well, now, that's not necessarily a bad thing."

He adjusted his cowboy hat, bobbing it slightly as a young woman hurried past, entering the dime store.

"Murphey still own this store?" Chase asked the balding sheriff.

"His son runs it now."

Chase nodded. Murphey's son, Jackson, was a year older than he was. He'd known him in school.

"New stores in the places of old ones. Not as many people, but not much crime either."

"That's why I'm here."

Jerry nodded. "I have to say, son, I'm glad to see you back. Always thought your family was good and hated to see your parents move away."

Chase had enjoyed moving away, getting to see the world, or so he'd thought.

It was funny how his world had come full circle. He'd only wanted to escape to the big city, and now, because of his daughter, he was trying to escape back to the small town.

"The cleaners told me that my uniforms would be ready tomorrow," the sheriff said matter-of-factly.

"Saw your daughter over at the school this mornin'," he added.

Chase glanced over at Jerry. "You don't have kids there."

Jerry's chest puffed out. "I was droppin' off my seventh grandchild. She's eleven."

Same as Sarah. Chase nodded. "Sarah is having trouble adjusting."

"Only been here a few days. Give 'er time."

Chase wondered if time would help heal wounds but didn't say so aloud.

"Which brings up a problem. Since I'm working days, I'm going to need somewhere for Sarah to stay after school."

Jerry's brow creased and he reached up to adjust his tan hat. "Well, now." He paused on the street and stared out across the way, lost in thought.

"My mother-in-law has been here helping, but she's gone back home now." Chase figured if the sheriff had grandkids that age, he might know where he could leave his daughter.

"My daughter is a stay-at-home mom, so I'm not sure what to tell you. There's that day care over on

Cheyenne Avenue, but then, they don't take kids after they start grade school."

"What about after-school activities?"

Jerry shook his head. "Not much here in town. We're not big enough. Of course, occasionally one of the churches is havin' somethin' but that's usually around the holidays."

Chase had forgotten about the fact that there were few after-school things for kids. Of course, he'd had a mom and a best friend, so he'd never needed any activities. Looking at it from a single parent's perspective though, in Fort Worth, he'd always been able to find something.

"I don't want to leave her at home, running the streets. That was one of the problems in Fort Worth. I want this time to be right, to start over and do things better."

Jerry nodded. "Well, son, have you thought about Carolyne Ryder?"

Chase blinked. "Since when does she keep kids?" He hadn't thought of Cody's mom.

"She never has," Jerry commented.

"Then why suggest her?"

Jerry nodded at a car that drove past. Finally, still watching the traffic as it crawled through downtown, all three cars, that is, he said, "I'm thinkin' Carolyne might be keen on the idea."

And that was all he was going to say, Chase realized. *Mrs. Ryder.*

"If you're considerin' it, then you might want to ask now." The sheriff pulled Chase's attention to him.

He saw Jerry looking past him and followed his gaze to see Dakota heading their way.

"Well, fancy meetin' you here," the sheriff drawled, smiling at Dakota before shaking his hand.

Chase brushed back his hair as the wind caught it. "Walking to work?"

Dakota shook his head. "I'm meeting someone to check out the building across the street. I wanted to find out a bit more about the price to rent it. My associate pastor mentioned it might be nice to have a youth center in the area."

"That's a pretty big building," the sheriff agreed.

Chase nodded.

Jerry, being his usual small-town self, added, "We were just 'a talkin' about youth and such."

Chase watched as Dakota's attention turned to him. Astute, Dakota lifted an eyebrow and studied his friend. "Youth are very important," he offered. He glanced across to the empty building Chase had been studying earlier. The large glass windows needed a good washing and it looked musty inside, but it was a nice building…if the price was right…

"So, where is Sarah going to be staying after school?" Dakota asked casually, zeroing in as he was so able to do. Dakota was good at reading people and knew from what the sheriff said, that was most likely what they'd been discussing.

"'Scuse me." The sheriff moseyed down the street toward a friend.

Chase hesitated and then motioned to a bench.

Dakota checked his watch, glanced down the street and dropped next to Chase.

"Jerry mentioned your mom might be interested in

providing some after-school care." Chase cut right to the point. He might as well.

He caught Dakota by surprise. "Really?" His lips quirked.

"If you don't think she'd be interested—" Chase began.

"I didn't say that," Dakota countered.

Uncomfortable, Chase shifted. Then he sighed. "I came back here half-cocked, thinking that country life would be just what my daughter needed and I'm sure it is, but then…" He ran a hand through his hair. "I had forgotten that there just isn't much here if you're a single parent and don't have a partner waiting at home."

He should have found a better way to couch that information. However, it was out and that was that.

The sound of the occasional car mixed with the singing of birds, and the whistling of the sporadic gust of wind filled the silence as both sat on the bench.

Finally, Dakota nodded, a slow nod, as if considering some long mathematical problem and coming to the conclusion. "My mom is certainly good at mothering." He paused then added, "And she has been at loose ends lately. I think Jerry might be right. That sounds like something my mom might enjoy doing. Let me call her and see."

"Now?" Chase couldn't help but be surprised at how quickly Dakota had decided on that. He'd thought it'd be a few days at least.

"Sure, why not?" Dakota asked.

"Sure," Chase hesitated. "Um, a couple of things."

Dakota glanced over at Chase and waited.

"Sarah's a good child but, well, she hasn't adjusted well since…you know, um…"

He didn't want to discuss this.

Dakota didn't say anything, simply waited.

"I think she's doing better here," Chase added into the silence.

Dakota nodded. When Chase didn't continue, he pulled out his cell and dialed a number.

Chase watched.

Looking across the street, he could tell when the other end picked up. Dakota smiled. "Hi, Mom. Yes, it's me again."

He paused and stretched his legs out in front of him. "No, nothing is wrong."

A hand went up to his hair and he ran it through the short dark strands. "Oh, I'm glad to hear she's adjusting. Yeah. Okay."

Straightening, he motioned to a man walking down the street and then got to the point. "Chase is looking for someone to watch his eleven-year-old daughter after school for a few hours each day. Jerry suggested you."

Dakota listened. He nodded. "Yeah…" then paused. "No, I don't see a problem."

Dakota glanced at Chase and rolled his eyes. "Yes, I'll tell him to stop by." He watched the man crossing the street. "Listen, Mom, my appointment is here. I have to let you go. I'll be home for supper."

He listened again and then added, "Love you too, Mom. Bye."

He closed the phone and dropped it in his pocket. Turning, he said, "I'm around if you want to chat more about things. In the meantime, my mom sounded intrigued at the thought of having a young lady in the house again."

Chase thought of yesterday's guest. "Er," he started, not sure how to approach the subject of the second thing he wanted to ask. "About yesterday…?"

Dakota nodded. Noting the other man was still out of hearing range, he whispered, "Do you remember Meghan O'Halleran?"

Chase shook his head.

"A friend from grade school. Anyway, seems she has come to visit. She needs a place to stay and will be living out back in the garage apartment."

"Is having Sarah there going to be a problem?" Chase asked, low, as the older man approached.

Dakota grinned. "Nah. My mom will handle it. Listen, she wants you to come by and chat, get a schedule down for Sarah and all of that. So, go by sometime today and see her, okay?"

Dakota turned to wave at the man.

Chase stood, too relieved for words that his after-school-care problem was being taken care of. "Thanks, Dakota."

Dakota shrugged. "Any way I can help. That's what brothers are for."

Chase knew he meant those words in the Christian sense. It was certainly nice to find someone who believed that and practiced it. He nodded and thought he just might go to church this weekend after all.

Dakota turned to the Realtor. "Hey, Bobby. Ready to show me the building?"

"I sure am." The man nodded to Chase and then turned his attention fully on Dakota as they started across the street.

"Chase?"

Chase heard Jerry calling his name and turned to see his new boss coming down the street, a frown on his face. He reached up to his shoulder and murmured something into the mic that was anchored there as he walked.

Chase started toward Jerry. "What's up?"

Jerry sighed. Slowly he shook his head. "That was dispatch lookin' for you. Seems the school called…"

Chase's stomach fell.

"Is it Sarah? Is she okay?"

Jerry frowned. "I think physically she's fine. The principal said somethin' about words and a fight and needin' to talk to you."

The fear turned to acid in his stomach.

Fighting?

He thought he'd left that behind in Fort Worth. All of it.

What had his daughter gotten into now?

With an apologetic look, Chase said, "Since we're done with the tour, you mind if I go? I'll report in tomorrow as scheduled."

Jerry nodded and then reseated his hat. "Go take care of the problem, son. We'll see you at work in the mornin'."

Chase nodded and, with a sigh of resignation, he went to find out just what had happened that sent the principal to the phone to track him down.

And he prayed it wasn't as bad as it sounded.

Chapter Six

"Am I interrupting?"

Carolyne turned from hanging up the phone and smiled at her guest. "Of course not. That was Dakota calling about having me watch a child after school."

Meghan was dressed in an old pair of Carolyne's scrubs, some she'd kept from ages ago when she'd worked at the nursing home in the cafeteria for that short time. Though they were still too big on Meghan's petite frame, at least they were clean and in one piece.

Meghan's blond hair was wet and curled in tight permed ringlets around her face. Self-consciously she pushed it back behind her ear, while the other arm held her waist.

"Was Cody worried about, um…?" Her eyes cut away. She hesitated, her voice dropping, "Having someone like me around a child?"

"Oh heavens!" Carolyne shook her head. Then she chuckled. "You are something else, Meghan."

Carolyne picked up her cup of hot coffee and headed

into the dining room. "Why don't you join me," she of-fered, not looking back, hoping that playing it light was the right tack to take with this woman.

She'd offered compassion and now she was going to get down to finding out about Meghan and maybe find-ing a way to help her.

She heard the hesitation and then Meghan came for-ward. Curiously, she listened to the way Meghan walked and wondered what had happened to her left leg to make her partially drag it.

Serving up some of the fruit and cottage cheese on the table, she bowed her head and said a soft prayer.

When she was done, Meghan was seated across from her. She dipped up her own food and then self-con-sciously put her napkin in her lap.

"A friend of Dakota's has recently moved back to town and has an eleven-year-old daughter. He needs someone to watch her for a couple of hours every day after school. I told Dakota to send the girl's dad by and we'd set up a schedule. I love being around people and think it'd be delightful to have her here."

Meghan shifted.

"And I don't want you worrying about the situation. Chase was here yesterday and helped Dakota." Caro-lyne didn't elaborate. "He knows you're living here. So, since he seems okay with it, I see no reason to worry. Do you?"

Though Meghan didn't say yes, Carolyne could see it in her eyes.

She smiled sweetly at the woman.

Lifting her spoon, she took a bite of peach.

"I feel I owe you an explanation," Meghan said, pushing her food around but not meeting Carolyne's eyes.

Carolyne wanted to hug the woman, but kept herself seated. Softly, she replied, "You don't *owe* me anything, honey, but it might help for you to talk."

Meghan didn't lift her head. The first sign that Meghan might be crying was a tear that dropped onto the tablecloth. She watched the young woman shudder and then fix her shoulders firmly. With strength of will borne out of some inner power, she cut off the flow of tears and then slowly forced her gaze up to meet Carolyne's. "I have multiple sclerosis."

Carolyne waited to hear more but nothing more came. When it didn't, she asked, "Is that what happened to your leg?"

Meghan blinked, nonplussed. "I remember my…but you don't understand…don't you know what that disease does to you?"

Agitated, she dropped the fork and her hands disappeared into her lap. Carolyne could tell by the way Meghan's muscles bunched in her arms that she was gripping her fingers together tightly.

"Your grandmother had it, didn't she?" Carolyne remembered a bitter old woman in a wheelchair, the woman who, Carolyne felt, had most likely broken up Meghan's parents, but that was all speculation.

"You do remember!" Meghan gasped. Carolyne watched as Meghan forced the words out through clenched teeth. "I don't want to be like that. I can't be like that!" She broke on the last word and her eyes filled with tears again, though they didn't fall. Meghan blinked over and over until they dried up.

Carolyne silently prayed, not sure how to answer her. What could she say? She didn't know enough about the disease to help her. She didn't know enough about Meghan's family situation to advise her. But she could see the woman was hurting. She would simply deal with what she could see. And what she could see was someone who needed to know that people cared for her and she wasn't alone.

She got up and came around the table. Putting her arm around Meghan, she squeezed her tight. "You have to remember that God is in control, sweetheart, and He won't put more on us than we can bear. It's our choice to choose how we react."

Meghan shuddered, then stiffened again as if to hold back tears. Then she whispered, achingly empty, "God? What does He have to do with this? He obviously has deserted my family."

"Oh, Meghan." Carolyne's heart throbbed painfully for the young woman. "Why do you say that?"

Meghan shook her head. With her eyes downcast, she twisted her fingers in her lap. Her breath trembled in and then out with a rush. "Because of my grandmother, for one reason. And my father left us for another. Now God gives me a disease that's going to turn me into a hateful monster like my grandmother. I'd say that pretty well sums up how God feels about me."

Carolyne rubbed Meghan's shoulder in sympathy as revulsion swept through Meghan. When Meghan's shudders eased, Carolyne spoke. "You know, the Bible tells us that the trials we suffer are for the perfecting of our faith. In other words, sometimes God allows us to go through things to draw us closer to Him. Other times it is for His glory that we go through trials. And still other times, these things aren't for any reason but an attack of the enemy. We don't necessarily know when it's an attack or simply a trial allowed by God, but we do know that we have to trust God. Tell me, Meghan, are you a Christian?"

Meghan shrugged. "I went to church once or twice when I was a kid. That's probably why God is punishing me." A fresh shudder ran through her body.

Instead of addressing her erroneous assumption, Carolyne said, instead, "Christianity is about a relationship, not about going to church. If you want to find peace, that relationship is the first place you're going to have to look."

"What do you mean?" Meghan asked. "How can you expect me to make peace with a disease like this?"

Carolyne smiled gently. "Because God loves you. Do you know He loves you so much that He knew, before the foundations of the world, that you were going to be born, you were going to break fellowship with Him through sin, and that you were going to need a redeemer. Just as He knew I would, Dakota would, and every single one of us would. He sent His Son, Jesus, as the price for your sin and for my sin. And He would have done it if you were the only one who had sinned, or if I was the only one who had sinned. That's how much God loves us. Jesus never sinned—He was perfect—and He died for you, to reconcile you to the One who loves you—not One who would punish you for missing church."

"I don't know." Meghan studied Carolyne, skeptical. "How does that have anything to do with my MS?"

"Well," Carolyne began, "first things first. You need hope and that's the only place I can think of where you can find hope." She squeezed her shoulder again. "I have a book about the very subject I'd like you to read." She grinned. "It's called a Bible. I have verses underlined and a list of Bible verses I want to give you. You read those and tell me if that helps your pain. And while you are doing that, I'll look up some information on MS."

"I know all about it." Meghan's voice filled with bitterness. "I grew up with an abusive old biddy who used to like to hit me with a stick whenever I was around."

"That was over twenty years ago, Meghan. Things change."

Meghan collapsed against Carolyne at that statement. "I only wish they could."

"Well, we've set out on a plan. You read, I research, and tomorrow we discuss. How does that sound?"

Meghan sighed. "I don't know. I mean…I was aimless when I came here, so I suppose anything is better than simply sitting and thinking about it. But maybe I should do the research?"

"You read those verses first. They'll help you more than sitting at a computer. Besides, you still need rest and when you're feeling better, we'll get you online, okay?"

Meghan hesitated and then nodded, visibly relaxing.

"Will you be okay staying out in the upstairs apartment?" Carolyne asked gently.

"I think I can manage the stairs."

"Are there any other symptoms you've been experiencing that we need to know about? Any medications?"

Meghan shook her head. "I get tired a lot and fall asleep sometimes just sitting there. I think I may be forgetting more than normal but that could be the alcohol." She bit her lip to stop the trembling.

"You know, it's okay if you cry, Meghan." Carolyne crooned the words softly, thinking back to how many times after her husband's death she'd sat down and cried. "Sometimes it's good to mourn a loss, a change to your way of life."

"I'm afraid if I let go, I won't come back."

Carolyne hugged her close. Carolyne felt they had talked enough about the subject. Now might be a good time for a change. "So, what do you think we should do next?" she asked Meghan. "I mean, obviously you don't want breakfast."

Meghan blushed. "I do need to go lie down, but maybe we could talk some more later?"

Carolyne laughed and stood. "I'll be waiting. The electricity is already on and I've put toiletries up there."

"Thank you." Meghan smiled. Turning, she left and went out the back door.

The yard was turning brown as everything went to sleep for the coming winter. The garden was dying, but still had a beauty about it. She looked around the yard trying to remember.

So intent was she on studying it, she didn't hear the car drive up or the car door close. The first indication anyone was near was his voice. "What are you thinking about?"

Startled, she glanced around. Dakota stood there, looking handsome and so in charge. She forced her gaze away, back to the yard. "I was thinking even though it's been more than twenty years, things haven't really changed much. There are still tall plants that aren't quite as tall now, and the latticework is new, but other than that, your place still looks the same."

Dakota walked forward and glanced around the yard. "You're the second person in as many days who has pointed out that despite the years things around here haven't changed."

"You see it all the time." Meghan kept her gaze averted. "You probably haven't noticed."

"On the contrary. I'm so rarely at home that I've never noticed."

She wasn't sure what he meant by that.

The sound of the wind blowing through the trees whistled above. She wondered what the man next to her was thinking.

"It's been a long time," he finally answered her question by saying.

She nodded. "I am sorry."

He touched her arm, a fleeting touch from behind and then his hand was gone. "Don't be."

They stood that way for a while, neither saying anything. Meghan watched a blue jay fly into a tree and then a squirrel run up the tree, scaring the blue jay into flight. She felt much like that blue jay and the MS the squirrel. It has sent her running.

"I remember that promise," Dakota finally said.

That brought Meghan around, and staring into those deep beautiful eyes. "You're kidding."

A small smile tilted his clean-shaven cheeks into a pleasant look. "No. If I remember right, you were going to make me eat a mud pie."

She groaned. "Oh no."

He chuckled softly. "My thoughts exactly. And I'll have you know, I was grounded for a week after that pie fell into my lap."

The mood was broken as he glanced at his watch. "I'm keeping you from something," she said.

"I'm running really behind, but I forgot some papers for my briefcase. I had to stop back by."

She stepped back. He stepped forward. "I want to talk more. Those were good days, back then, slower days."

"Yes, they were."

He glanced at his watch again.

She bit her lip in worry.

"Don't feel out of place, Meghan."

How had he known what she was feeling?

"Accept the hospitality and stay with us. It's a time to renew our acquaintance, for you to recover. We're here for you."

In embarrassment her gaze slid away. "I have to go upstairs." She pointed behind to the garage apartment.

"And I have to go."

"Well…" She rubbed her legs and turned to go.

He started to leave and she heard him stop. "And Meghan?"

She paused and waited, not turning around.

"You clean up really good."

Mortified, she wanted to run, and yet, she didn't. In a way, that was one of the nicest things she'd heard in a long time and something that made her feel, in an odd way, very special.

Without another word, she started up the stairs. Once in the apartment, she lay down for a short time, and when she returned to the main house, Dakota was gone.

Carolyne was sitting in the living room drinking tea. She smiled up at Meghan. "Glad you're back, dear. Are you ready to talk?"

Meghan shrugged self-consciously. Then she offered a tentative smile.

"Well, come over and sit—" The knocking on the door stopped her.

"Oh Carolyne? Carolyne!"

Carolyne sighed. Smiling at Meghan, she warned, "Brace yourself. It looks like we're not going to get much conversing done."

Meghan looked at her, confused.

Carolyne only chuckled and strolled to the front door. "Good morning, Mary. Margaret. How can I help you?"

The two women bustled in nearly before Carolyne could open the door.

"Is that woman up yet?" Margaret asked.

"She's got a name, sister. At least, I'm sure she does." She looked at Carolyne.

"Of course she does, sister," Margaret replied. "But do you know it? I mean, she wasn't in any condition yesterday, and if she's not up yet…"

Margaret looked past Carolyne and her eyebrows shot up. "Well! What a change. What's she wearing?"

"Sister!" Mary turned to Carolyne, her blue hair bobbing as she shook her head in apology. "She didn't mean that. We found something for her to wear. Yesterday, well, she couldn't very well wear that, now, could she?" Mary thrust out the clothes she held.

Carolyne bit back a smile at the age-old dress that

had obviously belonged to one of the sisters back in the forties or earlier. "It was very stylish," Mary offered.

"Doesn't look like she needs it now," Margaret harrumphed. "And what is her name?"

Carolyne sighed. "Ladies, please come meet a family friend." She turned and headed toward Meghan, hearing the two women shuffling along behind her.

She smiled gently at the shell-shocked Meghan. "Meghan, this is Mary and Margaret—"

"I remember you!"

Both women stepped back in surprise.

Meghan blushed at her exclamation. "I'm sorry. I—it's the smile—" she glanced at Mary "—and your eyes," she said to Margaret.

Both women beamed, any past transgressions forgotten at Meghan's inadvertent flattery.

"Well, now, child. I have to say I don't remember you," Margaret tut-tutted as she bustled over to Meghan and studied her closely.

"I used to play with Cody." Feeling the close scrutiny, she flushed.

"A young blond-haired girl," Carolyne supplied.

Margaret frowned. "Mud pies."

"Oh yes," Mary affirmed. "I remember that. A little girl and Cody were famous for waiting until we weren't looking and going out back near the alley to dig in the ditch to make mud pies. We were always shooing them out of there."

Mary giggled.

"They made a mess, they did," Margaret grunted. "I was afraid I was going to step in one of those holes and break my leg."

"Oh, sister, they weren't that big," Mary argued.

Margaret simply whistled as if ignoring her sister.

Mary frowned.

Carolyne thought it time to intervene. "Why don't we go into the other room and have a seat."

They headed into the living room.

"We were just about to discuss what we were going to do today." They all took a seat.

"Well, that is obvious." Margaret glanced over at Meghan, leaving them all mystified as to what Margaret meant.

"Now, sister," Mary argued. "Let's get to know her first." The pointed look she shot Margaret seemed to belie her words, making Meghan uncomfortable.

"What brought you here?" Margaret asked.

Meghan blinked, taken aback by the direct question. But Margaret didn't let up. "Obviously you thought Pastor Cody could help you."

"And I'm sure he can," Mary added. Mary followed her sister's gaze. "He and Carolyne are the sweetest people and such wonderful neighbors."

"Be that as it may," Margaret added, "you came here for something. That much is obvious."

"Now, ladies," Carolyne intervened. "Let's not put Meghan on the spot."

Margaret backed off.

The room fell quiet.

Meghan shrugged. "I have multiple sclerosis." Her eyes were downcast, so she didn't see the sisters' reactions, but Carolyne did. And Meghan certainly heard them.

"Oh, you poor dear!" Margaret stood up and tottered

over to her. And then Margaret did something very unusual for the sisters—she fell down next to Meghan and pulled her into a hug.

Carolyne watched, stunned.

"You must be devastated." Mary pushed herself up, tottering over to the other side. "I remember your grandmother."

Meghan burst into tears.

"Well, that's nice, now, isn't it, sister." Margaret glared at her sister.

"What did I do?" Mary asked and started patting Meghan's shoulder. "There there, dear. It's going to be okay. God is in control."

"Well, of course He is, sister. Don't I always say that?" Margaret made soothing sounds.

She reached over to the table, pulled out some tissues from the floral box and pushed them into Meghan's hand. "Now, here we go. This isn't the end of the world—"

"Well, of course it's not, sister," Mary began. "The Bible says—"

"I was *speaking* metaphorically." Margaret stared down her nose at her sister.

"She likes to think she's smart." Mary sniffed delicately.

Meghan wiped her eyes and then blew her nose.

"As I was saying," Margaret continued, "it's not the end of the world. You came here for help and help you are going to get."

"I—excuse me?" Meghan asked. She glanced to Carolyne for help but Carolyne had no idea what in the world the sisters were up to.

"Well…it's obvious you need clothes. So, first business of the day is to go shopping."

Meghan blushed and Carolyne was certain she knew why. Meghan had no money, she would bet, so she tried to intervene. "I have someone coming over later today. Chase needs a babysitter and I promised him I'd be here to talk with him about watching his daughter."

"Do you think that wise?" Margaret asked and glanced at Meghan.

"I see no problem," Carolyne said, "but since I have to be here, Meghan and I won't be able to go out and do any shopping today."

Carolyne thought she'd solved that problem until Margaret, with her ways, replied, "Nonsense. We'll take her."

"Oh, my." Mary clapped her hands together. "That would be delightful."

Meghan flushed again. "I—well—I don't have a job right now." She fidgeted, confirming Carolyne's fears.

Margaret studied her. "Spent your last penny on booze, did you?"

Meghan turned red to the roots of her hair and Carolyne nearly groaned.

"Don't you worry," Margaret reassured her. "We don't get to help people often."

"Oh, my, that's true," Mary added. "Why, the last time was in 1976, or was it 1986?"

Margaret frowned. "It was last February, dimwit."

"You don't have to name call," Mary admonished. "And that doesn't count."

"And why not?"

"Because the young person we helped ended up—"

"Still it counts." Margaret waved a blue-veined hand. "And you don't have to worry about paying us back," Margaret warned her. "Papa left us money."

"We're rich," Mary affirmed.

"We don't have anything else to spend the money on," Margaret added.

"But you don't know me," Meghan argued, looking embarrassed and a bit flustered.

Carolyne thought to intervene and then simply sat back and waited. She'd known the women too long and knew it would be useless.

Margaret smiled. "You need help, and we can help. What else is there to know?"

Mary patted Meghan's hand. "And we really want to do this for you."

"We need to put any rumors to rest about Pastor Cody and any bad morals going on here. The entire town knows about yesterday."

"Margaret!" Carolyne had to admit Margaret had shocked her with that.

"Well, you know how a town can gossip. And Pastor Cody needs all the help he can get."

A ghost of a smile crossed Meghan's face. Carolyne wondered what it was that the sisters had said that amused Meghan enough to draw that look. She had to admit the way Margaret had made that last statement so melodramatically nearly drew a smile from her as well. The sisters were very protective of Dakota and it showed whenever they talked about him.

"Well, if it's to protect Pastor Cody and his mother, then I guess I'll go."

"See! I knew you were a good girl. Didn't I tell you,

Carolyne? She's a good girl and wants to make sure no one thinks anything else!"

Actually, Carolyne thought, Margaret was the very one who had called her and suggested that Meghan was a lady of the evening.

"I believe that was me that said she was a good girl, sister," Mary argued.

"No. You told Carolyne she was drinking," Margaret corrected. "I'm the one who didn't call the police."

"Well, I didn't either. Did you see any police out here?" Mary waved her arthritic hand toward the front door, agitated.

"That's not the point." Margaret turned to Meghan and patted her hand, smiling as if she'd scored a point with her sister. "We'll go get ready. Come over to our house in fifteen minutes and we'll leave."

"You can drive?" Meghan asked, surprised.

"Well, of course." Margaret actually looked offended.

"But I'm the better driver," Mary added.

"No, you're not," Margaret disagreed, clearly exasperated with her sister. "You drove up on that curb last week. Remember?"

"I've never been in a wreck," Mary informed them superiorly, a smile curving her lips and changing the wrinkles on her face to lines of happiness.

"That was back during the war, sister," Margaret argued. "One wreck. One wreck and you think that means my driving is worse than yours. Well, what about that tree you nearly hit?" Margaret asked as she slowly pulled herself to a standing position and started toward the door.

Mary stood and creakily walked out after her, tottering along as fast as she could go. "That wasn't my fault. If you hadn't distracted me…"

Their voices faded as they teetered on down the stairs and toward their yard.

"Wow." Meghan shook her head in bewilderment.

Carolyne smiled. "They haven't changed a bit, have they?"

Meghan chuckled. Then her expression went from amazement to trepidation. "What if they were right and everyone knows about yesterday? I don't remember much. I just remember a bottle and laughing and…" Meghan bit her lower lip, her brow creasing with worry.

Carolyne was glad she didn't remember. And she wasn't going to admit the sisters were probably right about the entire town knowing. Instead, she asked, "Does it really matter what others think?"

Of course it did, Carolyne silently answered herself, knowing that they could give Meghan no end of grief. So she added, "Besides, do you really think anyone is going to notice you there, with Mary and Margaret in the same room?"

That ghost of a smile returned and Carolyne thought perhaps God had sent those two old women over just for Meghan. They had gotten her to cry and relieve the stress of her confession and had reassured her that they accepted her, and then when Mary had patted her hand in such a loving maternal way just before the sisters had left, she had seen Meghan melt.

They had accomplished more than Carolyne had been able to all morning.

Carolyne sighed, thinking perhaps she wasn't as

good with people as she had hoped, but certainly glad God had sent someone who could break the ice around the heart of the hurting lonely woman.

She had to wonder just what was going to happen in town. Seeing that Meghan was staring at her questioningly, Carolyne smiled. "I bet you'll have a great time in town."

Chapter Seven

Chase walked into the old-fashioned middle school, memories flooding back of years gone by. Tall narrow doors, no longer brown, but painted red and blue, with yellow and green full-length lockers, filled the hall.

The old ceramic tile had been replaced with new, light-tan tiles that shone with a recent waxing. But the smells were the same: cleaning fluid and chalk dust.

His feet echoed as he walked down the hall toward the office. Pictures of past classes hung along the left side of the hall as he approached the room he'd seen only occasionally as a child—the office.

Grabbing the handle, he pushed the door open and stepped up to the long counter where one man and two women were working.

He spotted Sarah in the corner, just outside of the principal's door. Sitting on the sofa, arms crossed mutinously, she watched him with a glare, though he could see through it and catch the fear behind it. Her blue eyes shouted that fear even as they tried to convey loathing.

Her fisted hands were a sure sign that his mousy-haired little girl knew whatever she'd done was going to see punishment.

Oh, yes, he knew that look well and she was braced for a fight.

"May I help you—Oh! Mr. Sandoval." The older woman that he'd met the first day he'd enrolled Sarah nodded gravely. "Mr. Zimmerman is in his office. You can go on in."

The man who had been filing glanced up, studied Chase and then shook his head slightly. Chase wondered what that meant as he followed the older woman with the gray hair to Zimmerman's door. The young woman at the computer smiled a knowing smile and Chase relaxed. Evidently, it wasn't as bad as he had feared.

Chase gave his daughter one of his displeased looks, and then walked into the office.

Principal Zimmerman was a short man, with a kind smile. He remembered that much from meeting him. In his mid-forties, he struck Chase as very interested in both the school and the children.

He came around his desk now with his hand out. Chase accepted it. "I came as soon as I received word. Can you tell me what's happened?"

Old scenarios came to mind: talking back to a teacher, not turning in homework.

"Please, have a seat." Zimmerman motioned to the two chairs in front of his paper-covered desk.

Chase sat down in one of the chairs and crossed his ankle upon his knee. He tried to appear relaxed, but inside he was a mass of jumbled nerves.

"Mr. Sandoval, I'm going to cut right to the point.

Your daughter was caught smoking in the girls' bathroom."

Relief flooded him and then rage. Relief that she hadn't been hurt, followed by rage that she would do something like that to her body. "She has never smoked before. And Jerry said something about fighting."

The principal didn't look as if he believed him regarding his first comment. "It was a verbal fight. The secretary, Mrs. Moriarty, should have said *verbal*. Between the teacher and the two students."

He pulled out a manila folder and thumbed through it. "Sarah's file shows a disposition to trouble at her last school."

Chase scowled, his cheeks heating up. "Well, yes, but she was in with the wrong crowd there." And he believed that. She'd been going through a hard time and had isolated herself. Others had come in to fill the emptiness and she had started acting out over her mother's death at the encouragement of those kids.

The principal stopped thumbing. "Was it by her choice? one must ask."

Heat crept up from the collar of Chase's shirt—heat from rising ire. "One must also ask why my daughter isn't in here to tell me what happened herself." He had liked the principal at first but was quickly changing his mind.

The principal nodded. "That might be a good idea. Before she comes in, though, I'd like to ask you if there are problems at home, something that might be causing her to act out."

Chase's jaw hurt and he realized he had it clenched tight. Forcing himself to relax, he replied, "She lost her mother to cancer."

"I'm sorry," Zimmerman offered and Chase could tell he meant it.

Chase's anger drained. The man was only doing his job, after all, and sometimes that job wasn't pleasant. "It's an adjustment."

"Have you sought counseling?" the principal asked, concern knitting his brows.

Chase shook his head. When he didn't say anything else, Zimmerman took the hint and hit the intercom. "Sandy, send in Miss Sandoval."

In seconds the door opened and a rebellious Sarah strode in, arms at her sides, hands held tightly against her thighs.

Chase could see the guilt in the way she refused to meet his gaze. She stalked over to the chair and sat down, hands still by her sides, clenching into fists, a sign of fear for Sarah though it might look like anger to anyone else but her father.

"I hear you have something to tell me," Chase said after the door closed, leaving only the three of them in the room.

Sarah's chin went up. "It was only smoking. Everyone smokes at my old school."

"You included?" Chase asked mildly.

She shrugged.

He took that as a no. If she had smoked, she would have acknowledged it. She had no trouble voicing her opinion when she was angry. And by not having the ammunition to back up this latest incident, she wouldn't answer, hoping to prod him to anger as well. She was really good at that.

"Miss Sandoval. I'd like to hear the answer to that, please," the principal said in a fatherly tone.

She averted her gaze. "Well, it was offered. I mean, everyone did it but I just didn't want to—at the time. It's no big deal."

"I'm afraid it is at this school," the principal rebuffed her. "We don't allow smoking or drinking, profanity, intimidation of other students, no chewing tobacco, though I doubt we'll have a problem with that habit from you." He smiled at Chase shortly and then returned a stern expression to Sarah.

"No, we won't," Chase added. "Nor will we have a problem with smoking again." He stared hard at his daughter. "Will we?"

She hesitated, but couldn't stand up to his stare. "No."

Chase turned to the principal. "What is her punishment going to be?"

"Punishment?" Sarah sat up straight. "I said I wouldn't do it again."

Chase turned to his daughter. "Just because you won't do it again doesn't negate the fact that punishment should be given for a guilty act."

Sarah sunk down miserably into the chair. "I didn't even inhale," she muttered.

Chase sighed as the principal tapped Sarah's folder with a finger. "This is a first offense at our school, though she has been here such a short time that this behavior doesn't bode well. And I don't want Miss Sandoval to think we allow things that other schools might not allow. It's all in the handbook. Those things we don't want to see at our school."

He stood and crossed to a cluttered bookshelf and

dug through it until he found a booklet that had Tiger's Handbook stenciled across the front. He sat down and laid the book on his desk. "Every student is issued one of these when school starts. I am certain you were given one when your father enrolled you. However, since it seems you've lost your copy, I'll give you this one." He pushed it across his desk, stopping just in front of her. "And since you haven't learned the rules yet, I'd like you to copy the manual word for word and turn it in to me next week."

Sarah goggled at the principal. "But, that's at least thirty pages."

"Thirty-two," Zimmerman corrected. "Will you do this at home or am I going to have to keep you after school every day until it's done?"

Sarah looked at her dad, trying to look mutinous but failing wretchedly. She'd already used up her measure of bravado today and was back to being a scared little girl who was hurting and striking out and now very worried about what might happen.

"She'll be able to do it after school." Chase didn't break her gaze. "Carolyne Ryder is going to be watching her each day until I get off work."

"A babysitter?" Sarah wailed in disbelief.

"Looks like you need one," Chase countered, his gaze hardening. "And I will make sure Carolyne understands how many pages each day you have to have done before I pick you up."

"But what about free time?" Sarah demanded.

"You forfeited that when you decided to break the law."

Sarah scoffed and flopped back in her seat.

He tried to reassure his daughter. "You'll like Ms.

Ryder. And if you do the work you're supposed to, we'll see about going from there with your restriction."

Sarah didn't comment. Chase looked to Zimmerman and the principal nodded. "You can return to class now. Have Mrs. Moriarty write you a slip."

She nodded and stood. Her feet dragged all the way to the door. Chase didn't comment until she was gone and the door shut firmly behind her.

"She was smoking?" he asked again, unable to believe it.

Zimmerman frowned. "Our history teacher, Mrs. Henderson, was walking by the girls' rest room and smelled smoke." Zimmerman shook his head. "These kids seem to think they can light up and we won't smell it. Anyway, she went into the bathroom and saw Sarah with another young person standing there. The other girl had the tobacco and threw the cigarette into the toilet. She flushed it, but she was too late because Mrs. Henderson had already seen her with it. Mrs. Henderson found a stash of cigarettes in the girl's sock—three to be exact. Halley is a troubled child and it worries me that Sarah has taken up with her so soon." He studied Chase and then asked, "You say she'll be staying with Pastor Dakota's mother after school?"

Chase nodded.

"I don't know the entire situation, and forgive me if I'm butting in." He leaned forward in his chair. "But I want to try to stop this behavior before it escalates. You might consider talking to Pastor Dakota, since it seems you know the family, ask his advice about how to help your daughter cope with loss. As for the school, we have counselors available and the children know this. Remind her of it so the next time she is feeling rebellious she can go talk to someone instead of acting out."

Chase sighed. "I think the idea behind rebellion is to act out, not talk."

The principal nodded. "Perhaps, but hopefully we can direct her energies into talking instead."

"It's been hard on her. I took this job here so I could have more time with Sarah. She's grieving and needs me at home more."

"It's good that you see that, Mr. Sandoval. Perhaps you're on the right road already."

Chase hated that all of this was being made so public in a new town. With a nod he stood. "I need to go talk with Mrs. Ryder. I'll pick Sarah up after school, so please send a note to her last class that she's not to ride the bus home."

Zimmerman stood as well. "I'll see to that." He stuck out his hand. "I hope we don't meet like this again."

Chase knew Zimmerman was an honest man. He could see it in his eyes. But he could also see that the principal had already pegged Sarah as a troublemaker and his words were more of a warning than a statement of hope. He shook Zimmerman's hand and wondered if his daughter really was in trouble because she chose to rebel or because she just kept getting involved with the wrong crowd.

It had to be the latter.

Turning, he headed out of the office to find Carolyne Ryder and set up a schedule with her to care for his delinquent daughter.

Meghan made her way up the stairs to Dakota's house. She felt as if she'd been run through the wringer and left hanging in the wind.

"Bye, dear!" Mary called as she and Margaret started up the stairs to their house.

Meghan started to wave and then remembered the cane in her hand. She shifted it to rest against her side and lifted her arm in acknowledgment before sighing in relief as the two older sisters entered their house.

She would never, ever allow either one of them to drive her anywhere again. If finding out she had MS hadn't given her gray hair, their driving had.

"Meghan!" Carolyne pushed open the door and only then did Meghan realize someone was standing next to the woman.

He looked vaguely familiar but she couldn't place him.

"This is Chase Sandoval. He was just leaving. I'm so glad you are able to meet him. This is Sarah's father."

Meghan studied the man. He was very nice looking, both rugged and handsome, but there was something in his eyes that spoke of grief—even as he smiled and extended his hand.

"You didn't have a cane the other day," he said as he shook her hand warmly.

She blushed as she realized this must have been the man who had helped Cody get her into the house yesterday. "Um, the sisters—" she gestured toward next door "—they saw me, well…I don't walk well, and so they suggested it, or rather, insisted."

Chase chuckled. "They can do that."

Meghan glanced at her feet, thinking the packages were getting awfully heavy.

Chase stepped out and reached for the parcels. "Here, let me."

She allowed it simply because she was still too embarrassed about the way she'd first met him to object. "Thank you." She started in behind him. "I want to apologize for the other day—"

He shook his head. "Not my business. If Dakota trusts you and says you're an old friend, that's good enough for me."

"Meghan," Carolyne admonished quietly as she followed her in, "you need to stop apologizing. We all make mistakes."

Meghan sank gratefully onto the nearby sofa and listened as Chase said goodbye to Carolyne and then departed.

When Carolyn returned, she clucked her tongue. "You look exhausted, dear."

Meghan nodded. "The stress of riding in the car with those two…"

Carolyne laughed, her voice tinkling with merriment. "I've had that experience occasionally."

Meghan awkwardly laid her cane against the sofa and then leaned forward. "I mean, Mrs. Ryder, they—"

"Call me Carolyne."

"Carolyne," she corrected and thought how odd to call this woman by her first name after so many years of thinking of her as Mrs. Ryder. But Carolyne's laugh encouraged Meghan to relax and confide in her as a friend, not as the parent of a friend. Seeing the anticipation in Carolyne's smile, she continued with the story. "Margaret went up on the curb at one point and crossed the center median—the grassy median!" She shook her head. "And she and Mary argued the entire time. When we got ready to come home, Mary was in the driver's seat. Margaret wasn't happy with that, but I was, until

Mary started driving. She was going down a one-way street—the wrong way!"

"Oh, dear." Carolyne covered her mouth with her fingers, amusement in her eyes.

Meghan nodded. "And someone, I think it was the sheriff, nearly got run over. Mary stopped to apologize and he warned her if she couldn't turn that car around he was going to have to ticket her. She informed him that he had only said that because she'd turned him down for a date years ago because he was too young."

Carolyne burst into laughter. "They are a pair! But it looks like you got some shopping done."

Meghan nodded. "They bought me too much. I just couldn't argue though."

"Didn't let you get in a word edgewise?" Carolyne asked sagely.

Meghan leaned back in fresh exhaustion. "And they can certainly go through the stores. They have some things on order." Meghan grimaced. "They seemed so happy and I guess I'm just a sap with them."

Carolyne shook her head and came to stand near Meghan. "They have a way about them, dear. So you've been feeling fatigued often?"

Her gaze slid away from Carolyne. She didn't like talking about that problem. But she owed Mrs. Ryder that. She had been so good to let her stay here. "Yes, lately. I do anything and it seems I'm exhausted. Well, anything more than normal. Walking a long distance or shopping for four hours…" She trailed off. "It's only been happening since shortly before the diagnosis of MS and I am wondering if it's related to the problem."

Carolyne frowned. "I'm going to get to that information as soon as possible. But since you're tired, why don't you go take a nap."

Meghan frowned. "It's the middle of the day."

Carolyne smiled. "Isn't that when naps are taken?"

"I feel, well, like I'm slouching if I don't at least help around here." Meghan shrugged with frustration.

"Meghan, honey…" Carolyne sat down and took Meghan's hands in her own. The contact calmed her frayed nerves, and Meghan slowly lifted her gaze to meet Carolyne's. "You don't have to do anything to earn your keep. Take a day or two and rest up. You've been given a horrible shock with your diagnosis and now a double shock that you're unemployed. Let's just give you time to grieve, to adjust, and then we'll go from there."

"But—" Meghan started.

Carolyne shook her head. "Think of yourself as a daughter. You can jump in if you see I need a helping hand, otherwise, let's take this slowly and give you time to get used to being here."

Meghan felt tears come to her eyes. She didn't deserve this sweet woman or her help. "Why?" she asked simply.

Carolyne looked at her. "Why not?"

"Because I don't deserve it. I'm homeless. I don't have any money."

"Shush…" Carolyne patted her hand. "Go read those verses I gave you and you'll see that none of us deserve it, but because of God's love we can give it."

Meghan didn't understand.

Carolyne smiled, seeing she didn't. "Go ahead."

The soft sweet voice won out and Meghan nodded. Wearily she stood and gathered her packages and then her "new helper device," as Mary had informed her it was called. Slowly, awkwardly, the cane feeling foreign in her hand, she made her way to the kitchen, out the back door, down the steps and to the garage apartment—the entire time thinking that life just wasn't ever going to return to normal again.

Chapter Eight

"The meeting with the contractor went great. He was able to give us the estimate we wanted so the youth extension is a go."

Dakota paused by the door to twenty-three-year-old youth pastor Jeff Dunnaway's office. Jeff glanced up from his laptop and grinned. "That's cool."

The man was young, enthusiastic, and on fire for God. His only problem was that he wasn't married. Dakota kept teasing him, trying to get him hooked up so that all of the young girls would realize he wasn't available and ease up with their puppy-dog eyes, but it just didn't seem to work out. Jeff was too dedicated to his job to bother with dating, just as Dakota had been for so long now. "I'll see that you get a copy of the paperwork to look over," Dakota added and turned to leave.

"Hey—" Jeff pushed his laptop aside before leaning back in his chair "—I have an idea I want to run past you for the next quarter. I've been praying about it and think it'd be really great for the youth."

Dakota glanced at his watch and nodded. "I have two appointments coming in but after that I'll have some free time."

"Great." Jeff pulled his laptop back in front of him.

Dakota headed toward his office, jubilant that things had gone so smoothly with the contractor.

If only it'd gone that smoothly with the real estate agent.

The agent's price was right, but the man had informed him that he was afraid the person renting out the building wouldn't want kids housed there. He was going to have to get back to them on that. Funny how those words had changed so quickly. Dakota had only had to go home and get some papers and in that short time the Realtor's attitude had changed.

Part of it was probably because Dakota had been so distracted. Meghan hadn't even looked like the same woman as yesterday. He had pulled up, seen her, and immediately thought someone had wandered into his backyard. It was only as he approached that he'd suddenly realized it was Meghan.

Wow.

She'd looked so vulnerable and alone, not like the sweet little girl he remembered. Of course, thinking back, he realized she had been very lonely back then— that's why she'd practically lived at his house. And he'd been one of her only friends because she'd never dressed the nicest or been one of the in-crowd.

Talking to her had made him want to stay and get to know her and end up spending hours with her. That could be dangerous since he had too many other things to do.

But it had been so refreshing.

And with all of that on his mind, he hadn't been very attentive when he'd returned to talk with the real estate agent.

Of course, if they couldn't get that building, then they would have to use part of the wing for the town youth activities they had planned—which meant they would outgrow the wing before it was even built. He'd really wanted that building.

He didn't want to think about that now. He'd bring it up at the business meeting in a couple of weeks. And he'd put his new guest from his mind for now.

"The Bennetts are here," Dakota's assistant said as he walked into the main office area.

"I see that." He smiled at the man and woman who sat just outside his office. "Come in," he added and reached out to shake the older man's hand and then his wife's.

Georgia and Zachary Bennett were descended from the town patriarchs. The Bennetts had moved here during oil rush days, helped found the town and been active in everything from simple tool stores to politics ever since.

He paused to hold out a chair for Georgia before going around his desk and seating himself.

The couple was in their fifties with four children and three grandchildren so far. Their daughter Emma was expecting a child just after Christmas. Georgia was elegant. There was no other way to describe her. She sat straight and regal in her chair, her blue pantsuit perfectly matching her blue shoes and blue purse. A strand of pearls graced her neck, and her makeup was flawless.

She loved social activities and taking all of the kids and grandkids to Dallas to shop.

Her husband, Zach, as he insisted on being called, wore a casual suit. He held the job of city councilman and everyone knew his opinion on everything.

They were large tithers and while he was glad for the money, Dakota knew that they were here to check up on how the funds were being spent. Being large contributors to the church, as well as on the board of elders, made Zach and his wife feel that it was necessary to come by at least once a month to discuss finances.

Dakota didn't mind, as the books were open to any church member. What he did mind was when the discussion changed to meddling or insinuating that because they gave so much money, they should be able to say how it was spent.

"Well, now, Pastor, I hear you had a meeting with the contractor today."

That was Zach Bennett—right to the point. Dakota leaned back in his chair and crossed his legs, resting his hands on the arms of the chair. He ignored the look that Georgia gave him when his chair squeaked. He really needed to fix that. Instead, he smiled. "I did. As a matter of fact, I just returned."

"And how did it go?"

"Real good, Zach. I'll be typing up a report and presenting it at the business meeting."

"I'm so glad to hear that," Georgia added. "We'd heard a rumor you had been over looking at the empty Wilson property." Her hand fluttered to her neck and worried at her pearls.

News traveled quickly today, he noted. Rocking forward in his chair, he uncrossed his legs. "Oh, no, ma'am. That's no rumor. That is a fact that I stopped by and checked out the property."

Things were beginning to make sense. He'd wondered why the real estate agent had been so excited to show him the property but then today had said it wasn't suited for youth. Someone, most likely the man seated in front of him, had put some pressure on the agency.

"Now, Pastor, I thought we'd discussed this and decided that property right there in the middle of town wouldn't be right for a bunch of hoodlums." He shook his head and tsked. "God may want us to reform them, but He sure doesn't want us putting our neighbors at risk."

Dakota was saved by the bell—literally. His phone rang. "Excuse me."

He couldn't be happier that he didn't have to respond to what Zach had just said. In fact, he had told the Bennetts before that the church needed to do more for the people of this town, including building a youth center where they could minister to the kids of the area. The Bennetts felt the church's money should be used on those in the church instead.

"Hello?"

"Pastor Cody?"

He nearly groaned. Mary and Margaret at a time like this.

"Yes, ma'am, I'm here," he answered Mary. He saw that the Bennetts were displeased that he had a phone call. Oh well, he thought, realizing he couldn't ever dodge the sisters when they called.

"...a sofa—after all, that other one looked like just everyone had slept on it. And this one will be delivered today to the garage apartment."

"A sofa?" He blinked and tuned in to what Mary had just said. "To the garage apartment? Well, um, sure, that'd be fine." What had she said and what did she mean about a sofa being delivered? He smelled meddling again.

"I told sister that I was sure that other one wouldn't be right to sleep on," Margaret informed him superiorly.

"You didn't think the one there would be comfortable to sleep on?" he repeated, trying to follow what the two older women meant.

Georgia cleared her throat slightly and then pulled out a hankie to dab at her face.

He held up a finger signaling it would be just a moment as he realized that the sisters were talking about their shopping trip today with Meghan. They had evidently gone overboard and bought a sofa for her.

He sighed. "I'm sure Meghan will be fine on the bed. There is a bed there, ma'am."

"Are you sure, Pastor Cody, that we shouldn't get her a new bed?" Mary asked worriedly.

"No, there's no reason for a new bed, but I do appreciate your concern—"

"We took her shopping today," Mary interrupted Dakota. "The girl has nothing. And to find out she has MS just like her poor dear grandmother. Who would have guessed?" Mary sighed dramatically.

"Which reminds me," Margaret added. "Your mama needs you home tonight to help with that poor girl. Are you going to be there?"

Feeling as if the woman was chastising him, he answered politely, "Yes, Ms. Margaret, I will be home for dinner."

"You don't want to disappoint your mama now," Mary added.

Dakota resisted the urge to sigh again. Glancing over at his appointment, he brought the conversation to a forced ending. "No, I don't want to disappoint my mama. Thank you so much for calling and I'll see you tonight."

He hung up the phone and smiled sheepishly. "I'm sorry about that. Mary and Margaret Mulgrew had some concerns and you know how they are when they're worried."

He well knew that they had taken Zachary Bennett to task over many things the man had done as a city councilman.

"Yes, I do. But they brought up a subject we feel we need to discuss."

He tried to think of what had been mentioned and drew a blank. What had he said that Zachary wanted to discuss with him? He braced himself for the answer, which was probably one of the real reasons they had come to see him today. "What would that be?"

"Rumors." Georgia nodded as if imparting great knowledge.

"More rumors?" he asked and smiled.

Zachary cleared his throat. "It just doesn't look good for so many rumors to be going around about the pastor of our church."

They always used the possessive when speaking of the church. That was good, as he liked people to think of it as their church, but in this case, their possession meant they felt they should run it, too. "Well, we can't control rumors, now, can we?" he asked mildly.

"Is it true you have a drunk living with you?"

Ah, he should have realized. The subject of their chastisement was going to be Meghan. "No, it's not."

He was being truthful. But not entirely.

"Well, that's good," Mrs. Bennett said.

"She's sober today and has moved into the garage apartment until she can get her life on track."

"Oh…oh dear." Mrs. Bennett started worrying her pearls again.

"We had hoped that one was a rumor." Zach Bennett frowned. "A drunk…"

Dakota shook his head. "She's not a drunk."

"Can you deny that she was drunk as all get out yesterday? We heard about the incident."

Dakota felt his temper rising, but he kept his smile in place. Folding his hands on his desk, he countered, "I don't go into the lives of the people of this town. Then I would be the one spreading rumors and gossip."

"Then you don't deny it." Georgia glanced away. "Oh, this is terrible."

"Now now, honey—" Zachary patted her hand with false sympathy "—I'm sure the pastor just made an error in judgment." Turning to Dakota, he added, "It sure doesn't look right to have a loose woman living on your property, you being single and all."

Dakota didn't say a word until he was certain it would come out nicely. Taking a breath, he paused to move some papers and then leaned back in his creaking chair again. "I couldn't agree more. That's why we're renting the place to Meghan O'Halleran. She has multiple sclerosis and needs a place to live."

Georgia frowned. "O'Halleran. Why does that name sound familiar, Zachary?"

"Is she the daughter of that crazy old woman in the wheelchair?" Zach asked, his face turning red when he realized he was right. "That old coot had MS, too. Do you know how much *time* of yours this woman is going to take if she has the same problem?"

Dakota sighed. He didn't want to think of all the time she might take, then again, with the compassion he felt for Meghan, he didn't think he'd mind making the time either. "My mom thinks taking her in is a great idea and so do I. Besides, she's not as bad off as her grandmother."

"Not yet," Zachary Bennett warned. "You'd better think hard about this. We don't pay our pastor to spend all of his time outside of church seeing to people like that. I mean, really, first you wanted to enlarge the youth room and we let you do that, but then you're wanting to bring in hoodlums to downtown and now move a sickly woman into your house?"

"Okay." Dakota felt he'd handled as much as he could. "I'll make a note of your concern and we'll see about it." He thought that a vague enough answer to get them to forget about it. He glanced at his watch. "Ah, Mr. Fredrickson should be here, so I'm going to have to bring our chat to a close. Was there something else I could help you with?"

Bennett puffed up like a blowfish and Dakota could tell he'd insulted the man. However, he was certain he was about to lose his sanctification over what the man had just said and thought the better part of valor was to cut the meeting short before one of them said something they'd regret. How in the world could these people judge Meghan before they'd even met her? But Dakota knew it wasn't really about Meghan, it was about anything that took away from his time as the pastor, anything that made him spend time in a way that Zach couldn't control.

"We expect you to finish this discussion, Pastor," Zach informed him.

"What is there to discuss? Meghan is an old friend that I've known my entire life. My mom suggested that she live in the apartment until she gets on her feet. Meghan recently lost her job and, since it is my mom's house, I imagine she has the right to say who can stay there."

Not to mention that he felt God expected them to reach out to the very people the Bennetts wanted the church to shun, the sick and hurting. But since he was trying to keep the peace in the church, he didn't throw that up in their faces.

"Perhaps I should have a talk with her then." Georgia ran her fingers back and forth over her pearls before finally dropping her hands to clutch her blue, beaded purse.

And his mom would politely and so gently put Georgia in her place without the woman even realizing it. "She'll be at the women's get-together Wednesday." He referred to the women's Bible study. "I'll tell her to make sure to chat with you."

That was his way of attempting to keep Georgia from going over to the house when Meghan was there.

"Oh yes." Georgia smiled.

Zachary frowned, and Dakota realized the man knew exactly what he was up to. He'd been as kind as possible, though he was certain his blood pressure was too high to be safe. He felt a headache beginning, and so he began to recite to himself a very familiar verse: *Peace, I give unto you, not peace of this world.* Slowly the tension drained, despite the fact that he still wasn't happy with the Bennetts' attitude.

"Honestly," he began in a conciliatory voice. "If you have any questions, I'll be glad to answer them. My next appointment won't mind waiting for a bit. But please let me reassure you that Meghan isn't going to interfere with my job. God called me to work with all walks of people, just as He called us all. If I don't help this woman, what type of pastor would I be?"

Zachary was in a quandary. Dakota saw it on his face. Finally, he grunted. "As long as she doesn't interfere with your job I suppose it's all right."

Ah well, what had he hoped for? Repentance of an attitude that the man had had since Dakota had first taken over as pastor at the church?

But from Zach that was as good as he'd get.

"It's just the rumors." Georgia's lips turned down in worry.

"I wish we could stop them all, don't you?" Dakota asked the woman.

It had no effect. She glanced past him, still worrying her purse. "It's just not going to look good. Oh dear."

Mr. Bennett patted her hand and she glanced back at him and fell quiet. "We'll just make sure there aren't any, honey."

Dakota thought that not possible.

"About that real estate property." Zach changed the subject back to what they'd originally been discussing. "Wilson doesn't want us in there, I'm certain. He's asking too much anyhow. So before you do anything, I think we need to have a meeting of the elders."

Dakota nodded. "That sounds good." He would talk to the elders and see what he could get done beforehand.

Zach Bennett smiled. "Well then, that's good." He stood. "We'll see you tomorrow night then. I'm looking forward to hearing a good message."

"And tell your mother I look forward to seeing her tomorrow," Georgia added, standing up next to her husband.

"I sure will." Dakota smiled and watched them leave his office.

Well, he'd learned quite a bit at the meeting.

Rumors were already abounding about Meghan. He'd have to tread carefully there, if Zach Bennett was to be believed. Zach had also blocked the real estate deal by calling in some favors. There would be no new outreach through the church—at least not now.

This town needed to reach out and give, but then people like Zach blocked it, afraid it would bring *those types* into the church.

He sighed and rubbed the back of his neck, wondering if the Bennetts realized that they all were *that type* and it was only the blood of Jesus that made them clean before God.

Nope. And they never would.

The Bennetts liked to make a lot of noise. Sure, they tried to make it hard for him when they didn't agree, which was most of the time he tried to spend money on anyone but the church body or time away from the church. They were a thorn in his flesh that he had to deal with on a regular basis.

Something else would soon come along, however, that would snag their attention and then he'd be able to find a building for the youth center and handle anything else that the Bennetts were currently arguing with him about.

That was the nice thing about having someone who meddled in everything. They were so busy trying to direct all of the areas of the church and his life that no area was ever concentrated on for very long.

So, he thought, sitting forward in his chair, Margaret and Mary still got underneath Zach's skin.

He smiled.

Remembering what those two had said, he decided he'd better hurry on to his next appointment so he could wrap up everything early today and find out just what all they'd bought for Meghan and the garage apartment.

If he didn't get home, they might have the entire place remodeled and turned into a hotel, he thought, grinning as he pressed the button to have his assistant send in his next appointment.

Chapter Nine

Meghan was exhausted.

It wasn't that she'd done that much—okay, a trip with the sisters was too much—for anyone. Still, however, she had taken a nap.

And now she was going to dinner, with company. Tapping on the back door, she called out, "Carolyne?"

"Oh honey, don't knock on that door! Feel free to come right in." Carolyne pushed open the door and smiled at Meghan. "Oh my, don't you look nice."

Meghan smiled shyly. She was wearing one of the dresses the sisters' had bought her. Dark blue, it nipped in at the waist and dropped to just below the knees. Her new shoes were comfortable and relaxed and she carried her clear Lucite cane. The sisters had been adamant about getting just this cane because it was a hollow clear tube that came with "fillings." Blue for wearing blue, black for black, roses for special occasions and jelly beans for the party look.

She'd laughed at the time, but she'd filled the cane

with the blue tissue paper and admitted it felt good that it matched what she wore.

"Thank you, Mrs.—Carolyne," she amended.

"I told you, didn't I, sister, that'd she'd look grand with that cane?" Margaret asked, coming forward. Her hands were covered with cooking mitts and she held a cake between them. "Should I ever need a cane, which I haven't yet, of course, that is the one I would like."

"Now, sister, I think it was I who said that was just the cane she should have," Mary corrected.

"Hmmph," Margaret muttered and turned to set the cake on the counter, grumbling something about Mary and knocking her with a cane.

Mary was whipping up icing as they spoke and simply ignored her sister.

"Our dinner guests," Carolyne informed Meghan. The doorbell rang. "And more guests, if I'm not mistaken," Carolyne added, her eyes twinkling. "Why don't you get into that top drawer there and set out the silverware, Meghan."

Relieved to have something to do, Meghan nodded. She felt the burning still in her leg from walking down the long flight of stairs and was actually glad she had the cane to balance her. Focussing on the silverware would help take her mind off her leg, she hoped.

The two sisters were currently engaged in an argument over how exactly to ice the cake, so Meghan quietly slipped out the forks, knives and spoons and took them into the dining room.

Chase and a young girl stood just inside the front door.

Meghan paused to study them. They were across the

room so she didn't hear all that was said. But she didn't need to. Their faces told the story. Chase was glad to be here though he kept casting anxious glances toward the girl who Meghan surmised was his daughter.

She shook Carolyne's hand politely but looked as if she'd much rather be anywhere else but there. Her gaze met Meghan's and she stared at the cane and then averted her gaze.

Self-consciously, Meghan shifted slightly to hide the cane and began laying out the silverware.

"Well now…" Carolyne walked into the dining room with Chase. "I know you've met Meghan, Chase. Meghan, this is Chase's daughter, Sarah." She indicated the young girl. "Sarah, this is Meghan."

Meghan smiled warmly at the child, thinking how hard it must be on her being the only young one here. Sarah stuck her chin up and said stiffly, "Nice to meet you, ma'am."

"And you," Meghan replied. She herself was ill at ease too and wished Dakota was here. Though she was quickly falling in love with Carolyne for the sweet graceful woman she was, she felt closer to Dakota, more at ease with him, as if he could protect her from the others she didn't know or who might expose her as a fraud.

It was silly, but true. Though she hadn't been back in years, she still felt an instant connection with her childhood friend. She wondered if he was even going to make it tonight.

"Hello, everyone," Dakota called, striding in the door on cue and dropping an armful of papers and books on a small table.

Meghan wilted with relief. All attention turned from her to the handsome, composed, smiling man who had just entered the house.

"Hey, man." Chase walked up to Dakota and shook his hand.

Dakota gripped Chase's hand in return and shook it. "I made it on time tonight, I hope, though it looks like everyone is already here."

Mary and Margaret walked into the dining room, pot roast and carrots nestled in white decorated dishes. "We wondered if you'd make it this evening at all," Margaret hmmphed.

"Of course he would, sister," Mary added.

His mom returned to the room with another bowl of potatoes and a smaller one of gravy. "You're just in time. Can you get the pitcher and glasses for me?"

Dakota nodded. "Of course."

He passed Sarah, ruffled her hair, and winked at Meghan. Though he'd put her out of his mind, he found with that dress she was wearing tonight, she was now back in the forefront. He was right, she really did clean up nice. In the kitchen he quickly washed up and then returned, carrying a tray filled with iced glasses and a pitcher of tea.

"So, how is everyone tonight?" he asked as they all took their seats.

They paused while he said grace and then Margaret replied, "We'd be a lot better if you would let us replace that bed Meghan is sleeping on. It's disgraceful, I tell you. Absolutely scandalous."

"I must agree with Margaret, Cody, dear," Mary said. "That bed has seen better days."

"Oh no—" Meghan began, her cheeks turning pink.

"I didn't know," Dakota interrupted smoothly and cut his roast. "I'll have to check it out."

"No, really," Meghan interrupted.

"Yes, really," Margaret argued.

"A bed is a bed, isn't it?" Sarah said into the argument, not looking up but cutting on her roast.

All turned to look at her. The room fell quiet.

Carolyne chuckled. "You are quite right. Except in some cases beds break down and become lumpy."

"I had a bed like that once," Mary added, as if oblivious to the simmering anger of the young child. "You've heard the story of the princess and the pea? Well, my bed had several peas the size of boulders. I was never so happy as when Papa bought me a new mattress. It was sheer heaven."

"They probably were boulders, sister. You used to get so dirty when you were a child."

Dakota shook his head. "I've slept on a few boulders—in sleeping bags."

Everyone laughed and Dakota smiled, until Sarah added, "I might as well sleep on boulders in this hick town."

"Sarah!" Chase warned shortly.

"Well, it's true. This town is small and has nothing at all." She glared at her father, her mouth trembling with anger as if she was trying not to burst into tears.

"You won't talk like that when we're guests in someone's house," Chase warned.

"Actually, it is a small town." Dakota worked to smooth over the tension. Both Mary and Margaret had that offended look on their faces and he knew if he didn't take charge of the conversation, there was no telling what they'd say. Meghan looked shocked and his mom had simply fallen quiet. Chase looked furious. "Many people leave because they don't like small towns. Meghan, on the other hand, has come back to visit."

No one could argue with that, so the problem was, hopefully, solved. "What did you do today?" he added.

Dakota noted the apologetic look Chase sent him. He nodded slightly in acceptance.

"Mary and Margaret took me shopping," Meghan's cheeks colored.

Ah, a faux pas, he thought, seeing Meghan's embarrassment. But the sisters weren't the least bit shy.

"Yes, we did," Mary said, her knife pausing over her roast. "And we had a grand time. We even stopped for ice cream."

"And you had a soda float," Margaret added, looking at Meghan. "Of course, I don't think you would have, had we not insisted."

Meghan turned redder. "You'd done so much for me already, ma'am," she said softly.

Margaret beamed, as did her blue-haired sister. "And we were so happy to for someone as sweet as you. We'll have to do it again."

"Oh, my, yes," Mary added. "I love going out for ice cream."

A strange look crossed Meghan's face. "I'll be glad to drive next time."

Dakota nearly guffawed but managed to turn it into a cough instead as he realized Meghan had experienced the sisters' driving skills.

"Are you okay, Pastor Cody?" Mary asked, concerned.

He nodded from behind his napkin and noted his mother's admonishing look. "Yes, ma'am. Fine, thank you. So, sounds like you had a fun trip."

Meghan nodded. "They bought me this dress. And thank you again," she said, her attention turning toward the sisters.

"Bah." Margaret waved a hand in dismissal. And so the conversation went, with the sisters filling in details of the day and Meghan being grateful.

Sarah ate in silence and Dakota wondered at it. Very few young girls were that quiet.

"Shall we retire to the living room for coffee and dessert?" Carolyne asked, and Dakota realized all were done with their food.

"Sounds great," Dakota stood.

He watched with surprise as Meghan stood and lifted a cane to her side. He had noticed her trouble with her hand as she ate and wondered if that too was from her MS. Her walking seemed more balanced, if a bit slower and awkward as she worked to use the cane.

He forced his gaze away and led the way into the living room.

"How was your day?" Meghan asked softly and he realized she'd come up beside him.

He moved and motioned her to sit and then took a seat at a right angle to her. As the others came in and seated themselves, he launched into a detailed description. "I met with the Bennetts today, as well as two other families, and then my youth pastor presented an interesting program he has planned for the youth."

"I like that young man," Margaret told him. "He's full of fire."

"And nice," Mary added.

Dakota chuckled. "He is that. He's a good guy." He accepted the dessert his mother handed him. "Thanks, Mom." Returning his attention to the people sitting around, he added, "Chase, Sarah might enjoy the youth group. They have several outings and are planning a winter one as we speak. You ought to stop by tomorrow night."

"I just might do that."

Dakota took a bite of the cake and smiled. "This is delicious. Who made this?"

Mary blushed like a young girl. "I did."

"It was my recipe," Margaret reminded her.

"But it was my frosting recipe," Mary added.

"Indeed it was."

"Well," Dakota said, beaming, "it was worth the effort, for this is one of the best cakes I've tasted in a long while."

Both women glowed. "You're such a good child," Margaret added.

Dakota watched Chase cover his smile and nearly laughed, until he suddenly noticed that Meghan was asleep. Cake plate in her hands, her head was leaning to the side and her eyes were closed.

His gaze on her drew the others' gazes.

"Oh, that poor dear." Mary set her cake aside.

"It looks as if we've stayed too long," Margaret added.

"She's had a long day," Carolyne said softly. "I guess we should have thought about that before planning dinner tonight."

"Nonsense," Margaret argued. "We'll take these dishes into the kitchen and then leave. It was fun. She needs to get to know more people and I'm sure she had a good time."

Margaret stood and Mary followed.

"Does that mean we're leaving?" Sarah asked hopefully.

Chase scowled at the way his daughter put it. "Yes, it does. However, I want you to thank Ms. Carolyne for dinner and thank her that you'll start coming over here tomorrow."

She didn't look happy about it but she did it. "Thanks for the meal and that I can come over here."

Carolyne smiled her sweet smile. "I'm so happy to have you, dear. It's been a long time since I've had a teenager in the house and quite frankly, I am very excited about having you here."

Sarah softened for a moment before shrugging in indifference. "I'm not a teenager yet."

"How true," his mom laughed.

The laughter caused Meghan to stir.

Dakota went to her and touched her shoulder. Long lashes parted and green eyes gazed up at him. In that moment, they weren't guarded or filled with the worries of the world. She smiled softly and met his gaze steadily.

Dakota felt an immediate connection just like this morning. He'd promptly removed his hand then, but this time he didn't, and he felt his reaction all the way down to his toes. He realized he was caught in that gaze, but that he didn't mind. She smelled good tonight, not like yesterday, but sweet and gentle, with a slight perfumy aroma. A strand of her hair brushed his hand where he'd touched. Unconsciously, as he watched her waking, he rubbed the hair between his fingers.

This wasn't the little girl he'd once known, but a grown woman, a very beautiful grown woman.

Amazed at his thought, he froze.

The shadow of fear and worry crept back into her eyes and she sat up. "What…oh dear. Was I asleep?"

Dakota regained his equilibrium and hid his emotions. He touched her hand gently, taking the plate from her. "I think it's bedtime for you."

Warmth spread through him when he touched her hand and it disconcerted him. Wow. He mentally shook himself. He was a pastor, and he hadn't had time for dating in so long that he'd nearly forgotten that feeling.

But it was there now.

He was attracted to Meghan. He didn't have to mention how wonderful she'd looked tonight when he walked in, as he was sure everyone had noticed the change. But it was her demeanor, so soft and elegant, much like his mom in many ways, which had captured him during dinner. He hadn't even realized it until now, staring into those eyes, how much she'd touched him.

He stepped back.

She shifted to get up. "I'm so sorry," she whispered as she stood.

"Oh, don't be, dear," Carolyne told her. "We're all tired and you especially. Don't forget our deal and we'll talk tomorrow."

She nodded and Dakota wondered what that was about.

"If you'll excuse me…" She turned to go. "Nice meeting you all," she added and then fled.

Chase walked up next to him and watched her go. "I think she was embarrassed about going to sleep on us."

Dakota sighed. "Looks that way. Hopefully she'll get over it. She did say her disease made her tired sometimes."

"What do you know about MS?" Chase asked.

Dakota shrugged. "Not much. Just that her grandmother had it and was in a wheelchair."

Chase nodded. "Well, I have to get my daughter home."

Dakota noted Sarah had already gone out to the car.

"About what she said earlier," Chase began.

Dakota shook his head. "Don't worry about it. She's hurting. She's going to act out. There's enough of us here to love her and help you."

Chase's look of gratitude was nice to see. "Thanks." He reached out to shake Dakota's hand.

Dakota returned the handshake. "See you tomorrow."

He nodded and left.

Carolyne closed the door after Chase and then turned to her son.

"Well, that went well, all in all, and I think we're building a good base of friends for Meghan."

Dakota nodded. He walked into the kitchen to help his mom load the dishes into the dishwasher. "I'm sorry she was embarrassed about falling asleep."

"She doesn't know us well, dear. It'll take time for her to feel comfortable just being herself around us."

His mom scraped the dishes while he rinsed and loaded. "I hope she gets adjusted quickly, because she needs a team of friends," Dakota muttered.

"Ah yes, I heard you say something about meeting with the Bennetts today." His mother didn't miss much.

He sighed.

"They had something to say about Meghan, didn't they?"

"They'd heard the rumors about her, that's for sure. And they're worried she's going to take up too much of my time."

His mother shook her head. "It's a shame they had to approach you so quickly about something like this. I don't understand why they're so afraid of change."

"They're afraid of losing money," Dakota harrumphed. "I don't mean that. I think sometimes that it's my age. I'm so much younger than our last pastor and I think they don't believe I can do the job."

He added soap and closed the dishwasher, starting it as he did.

"Hogwash." His mother waved her hand in the air in dismissal. "They're a tight, greedy couple who simply live to control."

"Mother."

"Well, it's true, and yes, I do pray for them, but there's no reason to ignore the truth."

"God can still change them. And none of us are perfect."

His mom nodded. "Just like little Sarah. Could you see the hurt in her eyes tonight? And the anger?"

"Chase has his work cut out for him with her. She's not over her mother's death by a long shot."

Carolyne's eyes took on a shadowed look. "Sometimes it can be really hard to get over a death, especially if you don't understand why."

She had grieved a long time over his dad's death and Dakota knew she had had a hard time coming to terms with why his dad had died in the granary accident. He had trouble sometimes himself. "We'll have to help her understand that God is in control."

"She's going to need a lot of love, that one."

"Well, I'm off to bed. I need some time in prayer and Bible study, and if I don't do it now…"

Carolyne reached out and hugged him. "I know, honey. Go on up. I'll get the lights."

He paused. "You know, Mom, I love you and appreciate you so much."

She chuckled. "I'm glad to know that." She waved him off. "Now go."

He shook his head. He didn't know what he'd do without his mother and her years of wisdom. He wondered how Sarah would do without her mom and vowed to spend some extra time in prayer about that and about the woman sleeping in the apartment behind their house.

Chapter Ten

The morning had been full of activities for Carolyne. At one point she'd noted the young woman in the dying gardens out back, a sweater wrapped around her as she walked to one of the benches and sat down. The wind whipped her hair and Carolyne had sensed her loneliness.

She'd left her alone, praying and waiting until she felt Meghan was ready to talk. Right now she felt Meghan needed some time.

So, Carolyne had gone to Bible study and met up with Georgia, who had questioned her at length about Meghan. Carolyne had grown weary of answering without giving information and was glad when Georgia had been distracted from the subject.

Then she'd had to go shopping, but she'd finally made it back home for lunch.

Meghan had fallen asleep, again, right during the meal, so she'd gone to her apartment for a nap.

And now Sarah was here.

Dear Sarah.

She'd arrived with a look of distrust on her face and a leeriness that made Carolyne's heart contract in pain.

"My dad told you, didn't he?" she asked, wording it, Carolyne noted, so that if Chase hadn't mentioned the specific homework, she could lie and get away with not doing it.

"Yes, he did, Sarah. Would you like a snack while you copy your work?"

She shook her head no. Then, "Like what?"

"Well, I have bananas and cookies and milk and orange juice. You name it."

She frowned. "I'm not really hungry but I guess a cookie would help keep my energy up."

Carolyne resisted the urge to smile. "I think it just might."

She went into the kitchen, got her cookies and milk, brought it out to the table, set it by Sarah and then she went to one of the chairs in the living room where she sat down. She picked up a packet of information she'd printed off from the computer. "If you need help or have any questions, feel free to ask. I'll be right here."

Sarah didn't answer.

As Carolyne reviewed the material in her hands, she heard the back door open. In moments, Meghan came in, hesitating as she saw Sarah.

"I'm being punished," Sarah muttered. "So just ignore me."

Carolyne couldn't let that pass. "There are results for our misbehavior, sweetie. Even as adults."

Sarah stared at Carolyne curiously and then at Meghan. "Are you being punished by God with the cane because you drink?" she asked quite innocently. Carolyne knew the girl had been serious when she'd asked Meghan that. But by the look on Meghan's face, Meghan didn't have an answer.

"No, Sarah. God doesn't work that way." Carolyne had to answer for her.

She saw Meghan shift and perhaps a bit of relief entered her eyes as she glanced toward Carolyne. "Come on in, Meghan. Have a seat. Have you read what I asked you to read?" she queried as Meghan slowly made her way into the living room and seated herself. A line creased across Meghan's face, showing she had slept hard.

"Those verses you had me read? God certainly punished that high-priest guy in the Old Testament if he went into that room and wasn't right with God," Meghan said.

So, she had read them. Carolyne smiled. "That's different, though, Meghan. In the Old Testament, the high priest was performing a specific ceremony. Remember, on that list, I mentioned things that are shown often represent other things? It's called types and shadows. Well, the high priest represented Jesus. I showed you the New Testament verse where Jesus is referred to as our high priest. Anyway," Carolyne continued, "the high priest's job was to, once a year, go into the place where God dwelt with the blood from the lamb he had sacrificed and sprinkle it on the mercy seat, which is the top of the ark of the covenant, so that we would obtain mercy for one more year."

"From sins," Meghan said. "Though I'm not sure how a lamb could do that."

"They released a goat sprinkled with blood to show that our sins were pushed off," Carolyn said. "Because, you see, the lamb couldn't actually cleanse us from our sins. It was looking forward to One who could."

"And if the priest didn't do the sacrifice right," Meghan added, "he was killed. That's why they tied the rope to him."

Carolyne nodded. "But how did they know he wasn't dead?"

Meghan shrugged.

"The priest wore a special garment with bells and pomegranates about the bottom. If they heard the bells, they knew he was still alive."

"That's what I didn't understand. Why does all of that matter?"

Carolyne smiled. "Because, these are symbols of things that were eventually going to come to pass. Jesus became that sacrificial lamb and died on the cross as the ultimate sacrifice. The lamb they sacrificed only showed their faith in believing a savior would come. Jesus was that sacrifice. Only someone who had never sinned could cancel out our sin and reunite us with God."

Meghan shook her head. "It's so much to take in."

"It sure is." She noted that Sarah was listening intently, so she continued, "The bells and pomegranates represent the gifts of the Spirit, such as healing, prophecy, words of knowledge, and the fruit is love, joy, peace, kindness and on and on. We see these at work in people's lives and it shows us that the sacrifice was accepted.

"Jesus rose, offered the blood to God in heaven, and

God said that it canceled out the debt. The Bible says that the wages of sin is death but the gift of God is eternal life through Jesus Christ, His Son. So, He paid the price, and all we have to do is accept that in order to start a relationship with Him and find ultimate peace."

Meghan sighed. "From this?" She motioned to her leg and then wiggled her hand.

"Yes, dear. From that. Your body shouldn't control what you feel in your heart. When my husband died, I was horribly devastated and not sure what I would do, but one thing I did know was that God still loved me, and even with the loss of my husband, I knew He was in control."

Meghan hesitated and Carolyne changed the subject. "Well, you kept up your end, and I have been on the computer like I promised and kept up my end.

Carolyne handed Meghan the papers. "Multiple sclerosis is a central-nervous-system disorder. Your body sees the fatty tissue that surrounds your optic nerves, your spine and your brain, as an invader and attacks it. Where your nerves are attacked determines what type of symptoms you'll have. For instance, since you are having problems with one of your legs, your spine is probably being attacked somewhere, I would guess."

"What do you mean, attacked?" Sarah asked.

Carolyne smiled, glad Sarah was curious enough to participate. "Meghan's body, for unknown reasons, has started eating away the fatty tissue that surrounds her nerves. And when it's happened and that fatty tissue is gone, her brain will tell her leg to move, but it'll take a longer time for her leg to get the message, if it gets it at all. If she's hot, the message takes even longer to get to where it's going, which means the muscles won't respond like they should. So, when she tells her leg to move, it might work fine until she goes outside in the middle of a Texas summer and then decides to walk five miles in the heat."

Meghan nodded. "I knew that much."

Carolyne reached out and took her hand. "There's more, honey. Some of the damage will go away. Give it six months or so to see. And they now have medications that can help slow the progression of the disease."

Meghan didn't look as if she believed her. "My grandmother wasn't on anything."

"That's because they didn't have them back then. They're called the A.B.C.R. drugs. Each letter stands for one of the four drugs they have for relapsing-remitting multiple sclerosis—Avonex, Betaseron, Copaxone and Rebif. A neurologist prescribes them. They work to slow down the progression of the disease and, from what I've read, a lot of women never end up in a wheelchair."

"Women?" Meghan asked.

Carolyne waved her hand. "And men, though it seems if you are a woman, you are twice as likely to get this disease as a man, and the farther away from the equator you live, the more likely you are to get it."

"Why is that?" Sarah asked, and Carolyne noted she had stopped working altogether and was listening intently.

"They don't know. And it seems if you are Anglo-Saxon—white," she explained to Sarah, "your chances of contracting the disease are much higher."

"So that's why you use a cane?" Sarah asked.

Meghan shook her head. "I have trouble with balance because of my leg."

"And that might clear up," Carolyne informed her, "unless there is permanent damage."

For the first time Meghan looked hopeful. "You mentioned that earlier. But how?"

"The fatty tissue grows back. Only if the nerve endings are permanently damaged will you sustain long-term symptoms. Meghan, it's all here in the papers I printed. You really need to read this and find out more about your disease. There is such hope, but you should be on medication."

"It won't stop the MS, though, will it?"

Carolyne shook her head. "No, honey. But with God and the joy and peace only He can give you, you will be more than a conqueror. And I'm praying that God will heal you completely."

Meghan shuddered. "I just don't know if I can live with this." She thumbed through the papers. Carolyne could tell she wanted to read about the disease but was afraid to at the same time. "I don't remember much about my appointment when the doctor told me I had MS." She shuddered and then whispered, "I can't be like my grandmother."

"And you might not. Over fifty percent of patients never end up in a wheelchair. I am so excited with what I read, Meghan. You have to read it as well. And I've included a bio on a woman named Sue Thomas, who used to work with the FBI. She has MS. Her story is wonderful. Read it and gain hope."

"You have so much information," Meghan said. "I'm not sure I can believe all of this."

Carolyne laughed and patted her hand. "Well, as I said, this disease isn't a punishment. God doesn't work like that. Discover His love for you, honey, and you'll realize that as well. And I think, once you read that information, many of your fears will be laid to rest."

Meghan hesitated and then leaned forward and hugged Carolyne. "You are a gift sent to help me and you have no idea how much you mean to me."

Surprised, Carolyne hugged her back. "I'm just one who knows what it's like to hurt and I want to help you get past the hurting. And if you'd like, I'll show you how to use the computer and you can research the places I've bookmarked for you."

She felt Meghan shudder and this time she thought it just might be excitement. "Thank you. That would be wonderful."

"What about making an appointment with a doctor?"

Meghan hesitated. She looked down at the papers and then back to Carolyne. "I think I might want to." She caressed the papers. "I just couldn't believe it when I was diagnosed. All I could see was my grandmother's face." She closed her eyes as if remembering. Then she opened them and focused on Carolyne. "Your words have given me hope just like those verses you gave me helped me find peace."

Carolyne smiled.

"I might actually be able to work again, to live again."

Carolyne took her hand. "Well, first things first. One of the ways to conquer fear is to learn all you can about the problem. Read up on that. Oh, and by the way, the most common symptom of MS is fatigue."

Meghan chuckled.

"Are you going to die from MS?" Sarah asked.

Both women turned at the little girl's voice they heard. Sarah sat at the table and she was no longer looking at them but writing again and purposely squinting at her paper.

"The information says that people with MS don't die from MS."

"My mom died. And they said people don't always die from cancer."

Carolyne went to the young girl and squatted down next to her. Hugging her with an arm around her shoulders, she said, "And people work in granaries all the time and never die, until something goes wrong. Sometimes we don't have the answers, sweetie, to why someone we love dies. But, think of it like a checkers game. Do you play checkers?"

Sarah nodded.

"Well, you can see all the pieces and where to move them to set them up so they can jump each other right?"

Sarah nodded again. "Yeah."

"Well, in life, sometimes we can't see why things are happening. But God can. Like in that checkers game He knows that maybe someone might stop serving Him later and turn away from Him, so He brings them home early, or He sees that if this person comes home early, other people will come to know Him. It's like a big checkerboard and God knows that this one thing must happen so that everything else will fall into place."

"So God killed Mom?" Sarah asked, aghast.

"No!" Carolyne squeezed Sarah tightly. "Sin came into the world. With that, sickness and death came into the world. God doesn't give us diseases, but sometimes He will allow us to go through a disease because He knows it's going to save someone else or help someone else to love Him. We were born to love Him and our life here is very short. You know the Bible from church, honey. Paul tells us that to live is Christ but to die is gain. In other words, he lives every day for God, but if he dies, that's even better because he will be with God.

"So, though your mom's death was horrible and is sad to us, God knows why He had to bring her home and we just have to love Him and know that we'll see her again one day."

Tears welled up in Sarah's eyes. "I don't want her gone though!" She jumped up and ran from the room. The sound of the bathroom door slamming echoed in the silence.

Carolyne stood, hesitated and then sat back down. "Oh dear."

"Do you think she understands?" Meghan asked.

Carolyne shook her head. "No. None of us understands. We just have to accept and go on and trust God. I'd better go to her."

She stood again.

Meghan stood. "Let me."

Carolyne was surprised by Meghan's offer. But she didn't argue. She nodded and sat back down.

Meghan walked slowly down the hall to the bathroom. When she got to the door, she knocked.

Sarah didn't answer.

Poor little girl.

Meghan pushed open the door and found Sarah sitting on the floor, toilet paper in her hand as she wiped her eyes.

Meghan ignored the glare the little girl gave her and walked in, closing the door behind her.

Suddenly, she wondered why she was there. What had possessed her to get involved?

But she knew. Deep down inside her, she knew.

Going over, she sat down next to the young girl, allowing her body to slide down the wall until she was resting next to the girl. She didn't say anything for a long time.

Neither did Sarah.

Eventually, she whispered, "Life's the pits sometimes, isn't it?"

The little girl shuddered and nodded. "I want my mama back."

Meghan nodded. "I wanted my daddy back too."

Sarah looked up at her. Meghan saw it from the corner of her eye. "He left and I never saw him again and it hurt really bad."

Sarah sniffled and wiped a sleeve-covered arm across her nose.

Meghan slipped an arm around her. "I feel all alone sometimes even now."

Sarah leaned up against Meghan, and Meghan wilted when she felt tears against her side.

Meghan realized she had started crying too, silent tears, running down her cheeks. "You have your daddy."

"Sometimes," the girl muttered, stiffening.

Meghan wasn't going to touch that comment, as she didn't know what was going on. "I guess we'll have to share Ms. Carolyne. She's really worried about you. She has a special love, I think. She takes in people who need loving and loves them."

Sarah, obviously getting over her tears, pushed away. "I don't need love because I have my dad's love."

Meghan smiled. "Everyone needs love."

As she said that, she thought about what Carolyne had told her about God. God loved her. He had given people an entire Bible showing His plan for humans and, if Carolyne was to be believed, it was because God loved her, loved Carolyne, loved Sarah and even had loved Meghan's grandmother.

Everyone needed love.

That meant her as well.

But could God really love her?

He hadn't done this to her. But she felt in some ways she deserved it for hating her grandmother so much. The material she'd read over said the disease wasn't really passed through families.

So why did she end up with this if it wasn't genetic?

Could she even love God?

Could God keep her from ending up a bitter old woman like her grandmother?

So many questions.

"I have to go finish my homework."

Meghan glanced at the now-composed Sarah and frowned. "It's okay to cry."

"I don't need to cry."

"Well, I'm here and so is Ms. Carolyne, if you want to talk."

Her young eyes averted and she stood. "Don't tell anyone the stuff I said."

Meghan nodded.

Had she helped the young girl any? Meghan wondered as she worked to get up off the floor. She saw Sarah glance back at her, hesitate and then scamper off.

The look in her eye of longing to come back in told Meghan she had made contact on some level.

More than that, talking with the girl had helped her. It felt good to help someone else and not think about her disease.

Glancing up toward the ceiling, she asked, "God, can You really help me?"

There was no answer. She hadn't expected one.

She was going to go back and reread those scriptures with the information Carolyne had given her and then read up on her disease.

Maybe there was hope in her future after all.

Chapter Eleven

Meghan rushed into the living room, patting her hair as she hurried along. She didn't have her cane today as she was walking pretty well.

It had been nearly a week since she'd talked with Carolyne and each day they had discussed more about the Bible.

The rest of the time, Meghan had secluded herself in the apartment, studying and researching information about MS and reading in the Bible about hope.

She hadn't gone to church with them on Sunday—she was still a bit too afraid to do that. She remembered the looks of some of the people in town when she'd gone shopping that day with Mary and Margaret.

It wasn't that they were bad looks. But some had stared. She thought others had probably decided she was inebriated by the way she'd walked, and then when Mary and Margaret had bought her the cane and made such a big production of showing her how to use it, she'd seen looks of pity in some people's eyes.

She was just Meghan. Plain old Meghan. But to them she was a drunk or a sick person or someone to be pitied.

The emotions she felt confused her and she wasn't sure how to react. Did she feel guilty that they were right? She was a drunk, or at least she had been right after her diagnosis. Was she despondent over the MS? She was angry that people pitied her, but hadn't she been pitying herself when she'd gotten drunk? Hadn't she only focused on the disease and refused to hear the hope?

She wanted to explain to them that she was sick but she was still the same person.

So she had called and made an appointment with a neurologist. She couldn't believe she'd done it, but she had.

She hadn't gone to church, and hadn't left the house, for that matter, since that day, but it had been time well spent.

And then Carolyne had convinced her perhaps a smaller group, like the women's Bible study, would be best to start out in. It had less than thirty women and was a very friendly, low-key affair. They were studying the tabernacle right now and after all of the verses Carolyne had given her regarding that building, Meghan was convinced she should go. She couldn't believe that every single thing in that building had meanings of Christ shadowing it. That had blown her away, but she still had so many questions.

If she weren't going for that reason alone, she would admit that she felt she owed Carolyne for all she had done.

Carolyne hadn't once looked down on her. Instead,

she'd quietly encouraged Meghan to talk, and talk Meghan had. She had made Meghan feel as if she were at home, part of the family, and accepted.

She had made Meghan feel loved—a feeling she hadn't felt in years. She had even made Meghan feel as if she just might be able to go out and face the looks she'd received on the streets that day—as long as Carolyne was by her side.

Not that she didn't have butterflies in her stomach. She did.

But it had to be done. She couldn't keep hiding, as Margaret had informed her only yesterday when she and Mary had come with more packages for her. She had to get out and face that fear, or that fear was going to eat her up. And those two old women were right. Though they liked to argue and were definitely a bit eccentric, they had wisdom that spoke to Meghan's heart.

So she'd agreed to go today to Bible study.

"There you are," Carolyne's smile was forever in place. She had just gathered her purse and keys and was getting ready to leave. She wore a pair of khaki pants with a button-up top. Her hair, turning silver, was combed back and curved under around her neck with a slight puff about her face. She looked very attractive and stylish.

She wore little makeup, but really didn't need it as her face glowed with an inner peace and happiness that Meghan envied. To finish off the outfit, she wore a pair of brown loafers. She looked as if she wanted to kick about the house rather than go to church. "Am I overdressed?" Meghan asked.

Meghan had dressed a bit more formally with a

brown skirt and long-sleeve silk blouse, hose and dress shoes.

Carolyne shook her head. "You look wonderful, dear. We dress however we feel comfortable at church. Some women wear dresses and others wear jeans. We're not particular here."

Meghan hesitated.

"What is it, honey?" Carolyne asked and her brow creased with concern.

"I just, well, I'm nervous."

Carolyne nodded, her eyes full of understanding. "That's why we want to take small steps."

"But what about the gossip? Do you think this is going to hurt Dakota?" She hadn't seen him all week. Late, after she was in bed, she'd hear his car pull up and many mornings he was gone before she came down for breakfast. He worked too hard and she didn't want to add to his burden with her reputation.

"Let Dakota worry about Dakota, honey."

Meghan couldn't help but be worried.

"Come on. Show them what you're made of." Carolyne started toward the door.

"If I knew, maybe I could."

Carolyne waited for Meghan to exit and then locked the door. They climbed into the station wagon and put their seat belts on. "You'll discover yourself as you have time to heal."

As they drove, Meghan found herself relaxing and enjoying the morning. The last of the leaves were falling from the trees and the wind whipped them along. She had forgotten how much wind there was in such an open city. The air was chilly. She'd needed something on her arms and was glad for the long sleeves. The air was fresh here, not polluted like in the big city and she found that she enjoyed the evenings and mornings outside, inhaling the scents of small-town America.

She could see for miles just outside the city if she would venture that far. And the stars at night were so bright. It was so different. She didn't remember Shenandoah being like this. Of course, she'd been five when they left. This was breathtaking. How she loved it, and loved this woman for everything Carolyne had done for her since she'd arrived.

Cars chugged about the streets while people hurried from store to store. And yet, despite all the hustle and bustle of the harvest season, the town was still quaint and peaceful.

As they drew nearer to the church, Meghan saw Chase standing on the corner writing up an accident.

A small sporty red car and a white compact sat back to front as if the white compact had stopped at the light and the red sports car had bumped it. Both were dented but no one seemed to be hurt. Another officer directed traffic around the accident. Chase saw them and waved, and then glancing about, he started across the street toward them.

Carolyne checked her rearview mirror and then slowed down. Smiling, she rolled down her window. "Good morning."

"Morning." Chase walked over to the car, slipping the clipboard under his arm. Leaning down so he could look inside, he asked, "Where are you off to?"

"Bible study," Carolyne replied. Chase touched his hat in acknowledgment of Meghan.

Meghan nodded. "Hi." He was a nice-looking man

and had a good attitude too. But she was still embarrassed that a police officer had seen her drunk, and was unsure how to act around him.

"So, how is Sarah doing?" Chase's attention had returned to Carolyne.

"She's doing fine. She mentioned that you were remodeling the house."

Chase shook his head and chuckled. "I'm only thinking about it."

"I'd forgotten you were a carpenter before you headed to the big city." The sound of cars passing on the damp road from a rain the night before was rhythmic as one by one they drove past.

"That was a long time ago." He shifted his stance. "So, Sarah's talking more then?"

Carolyne smiled. "Just give her time, Chase. She's coming around."

"I really appreciate all you're doing for her," Chase said. "By the way—" he pulled the clipboard from under his arm as he got ready to go back to work "—I'll be getting off early today, so she might not be at your place after school."

Carolyne reached over to roll up her window. "Thanks for letting me know."

"See ya." He hunkered back down and smiled at Meghan. "Have a good day."

"Thanks," Meghan murmured.

Carolyne turned back to the light, waiting for it to turn green. "That's nice he's getting off early," Carolyne said.

That brought up a subject Meghan wanted to ask about. "Dakota puts in a lot of hours, doesn't he?"

Carolyne glanced at her briefly before the light turned green and she continued down the street. "Yes."

"I don't mean anything by asking. I just noticed that he comes home many times after I'm in bed and is gone a lot of mornings when I get up. I didn't know pastors put in those types of hours."

Carolyne sighed. "I think he puts in too many hours, Meghan. But that's a mother's opinion." She hesitated and then added, "If he could hire an associate pastor to help with the load or even have some volunteers, it might give him more time to spend at home. His new youth pastor is great, but he needs an associate." She shook her head. "But that's not how it works, so he puts in extra hours to get everything done."

With a flash of insight, Meghan suddenly realized Carolyne was a very lonely woman, without a driving purpose in life. She had noticed that Carolyne always had dinner ready, waiting for Dakota even if he didn't show up.

It hadn't dawned on her until now just how empty Carolyne's life must be, nothing to do but knock around an empty house and wait for a son who never showed up.

"But at least he's doing God's work," Carolyne said and her melancholy gaze was gone, replaced by the normal perky Carolyne whom Meghan had come to recognize this last week.

Her comment about God's work brought about another question that Meghan had been pondering. She'd been spending many nights up, thinking about all she and Carolyne had discussed. Every day they would sit down and talk about the verses she'd read as well as the new information she and Carolyne had found on multiple sclerosis. She felt as if she were in school again, though this time she was enjoying it. "Is that what God is about? Doing work for Him?"

"Not at all. First and foremost, it's about a relationship. For example, a husband and wife have a relationship. They talk, eat together, sleep in the same bed, and spend much of their time together. The same is true of God. God wants a relationship with us. He wants to talk with us, worship together—He wants to spend time with us. But it all starts with that commitment in our heart."

They turned into the church parking lot. Meghan hurried on with what she wanted to say. "I read about how God chased Jacob all over the place until he crippled him and then finally Jacob became Israel."

"That's a very good point." Carolyne put the car into park and turned off the engine. "God loved Jacob and He wanted Jacob to serve Him. He didn't give up on Jacob."

"I keep thinking about that type of love, how wonderful it must be. God sent His Son to die for us, and He is willing to chase us down because He loves us so much. And with everything you've shown me, there's no way I can say Jesus isn't real." She thought of the many different historians and eyewitnesses that she'd read about in the various notes from various books. She shrugged and then admitted, "Even if you hadn't shown me the evidence, my heart tells me Jesus is real."

Meghan trembled and turned toward Carolyne. It took everything she had to say what she wanted to say next. She had been thinking about it for two days now and she just couldn't ignore the longing within her anymore. "I want that love in my heart, Carolyne."

Carolyne smiled the gentlest of smiles Meghan had ever seen. And then she reached out, took Meghan's hands in hers and said, "All you have to do is ask."

And that is exactly what Meghan did, right there in the car with Carolyne. She asked Jesus to come into her heart.

Chapter Twelve

Carolyne was happy. As they walked into the church, she admitted that the joy in getting to pray with someone when they accepted Jesus was probably the best feeling in the world.

"Hi, Mom. Meghan."

Dakota walked up the carpeted aisle, papers in hand, as if he was on his way out. Carolyne smiled at her son. He looked tired today, dark circles starting to develop under his eyes. However, when those tired eyes turned to Meghan, they brightened, Carolyne noted with surprised interest.

"Hello, honey," Carolyne replied, watching the emotions that played across her son's face before his gaze turned back to her.

Carolyne also saw the pink that entered Meghan's cheeks.

She wondered how she had missed this over the past week when they'd been together. "Meghan has some wonderful news," Carolyne prompted when Meghan glanced her way.

Her son smiled and waited.

"I—um—well, I asked Jesus into my heart."

Dakota looked speechless and then grinned. Snagging her, he suddenly pulled her into his arms and engulfed her in a bear hug.

Carolyne had never seen her son react quite that way with anyone over any news.

"I'm so happy for you, Meghan!" He hugged her longer than was necessary before he finally released her and stepped back.

Meghan stepped back, too, flustered but happy. Running her hands down the front of her legs and eyes shining, she said, "I don't know if I feel different or not, but inside I think there is a peace that I can't explain."

Dakota, still grinning, replied, "Everyone has a different experience." He checked his watch and the smile left. "I have to get these papers to someone but I want to talk later."

Carolyne frowned at her son, and how the interplay between Meghan and Dakota was forgotten at such a much-used phrase. "You often say that."

He had the grace to look guilty. "I promise. This time. I'll be home early tonight and I want to hear the entire story."

His gaze returned to Meghan and the attraction in his eyes was gone. He took her hand and squeezed it. "Thanks for sharing."

Eyes still shining, Meghan nodded.

Carolyne wasn't sure how she felt about what she'd seen pass between the two. One thing was certain, however: she didn't think her son realized how much he actually cared for this woman—and as more than someone to help. She had just seen the evidence. And watching Meghan's face, she feared Meghan was already half in love with her son.

Worries about Meghan at this stage in her new walk warred with how any rejection by her son could hurt her. Satan could certainly use something like that to cause her to stumble. Of course, with so many new things in Meghan's life, Carolyne had to wonder if the young woman was even ready to be looking at a man as she had Dakota.

Then there was Dakota. He was so busy. Could he find time for a relationship? Did he even want to? He rarely dated, too busy with life to bother, he often said.

But then Carolyne reminded herself that God was in control and it was in His hands. Both her son and Meghan were old enough to handle whatever took place, and Carolyne would simply be there to help if things went awry.

"Where do we go?" Meghan asked, and Carolyne realized she'd been standing there studying her retreating son.

"Through the door to the right of the pulpit. It leads to the offices and extra classrooms." Carolyne led the way. "I don't want you to be nervous. Remember, most of these women are nice. But we all have our faults."

"I'm not sure how that makes me feel," Meghan chuckled nervously, making Carolyne realize that instead of encouraging Meghan, she had done the exact opposite.

Working to reassure her, she offered information.

"You'll enjoy the study. We're on the golden laver, which represents the daily washing the priests did. Its spiritual significance is daily Bible reading and how we need to look into the Bible and wash ourselves with the Word. But enough of that. They'll go into more detail in the class. We also have refreshments. Coffee, tea and usually some sort of snack, so feel free to help yourself. And don't feel you have to share anything with anyone if you don't want to when we have our share time."

They got to the door and Carolyne pushed it open. She noted half a dozen ladies sitting about the oblong white table and chatting. More, Carolyne realized, stood over near the concessions. And of course, the very one she had hoped wouldn't show up today was there. Georgia Bennett. Georgia rarely missed a meeting of any kind at the church. And of course, with Meghan around, she'd want to keep up on anything going on. This was evidenced by the way Georgia spotted Meghan immediately as if she'd been watching the door and lying in wait. She started toward them.

Just great. Though exasperated, Carolyne pasted a smile on her face. She slipped her arm through Meghan's arm and held her closer.

Startled, Meghan glanced at her, but before she could say anything, Georgia arrived.

"Good morning, Carolyne. How are you?"

Dressed all in gray, Georgia Bennett looked elegant as always, right from the tiny clip she wore in her styled hair, past the white pearls, to the expensive leather shoes on her feet. She always matched perfectly. The scent of expensive perfume drifted to Carolyne, and Georgia's makeup, barely visible, was impeccable. Carolyne smiled politely. "I'm doing well, and you?"

"Fine." Pleasantries done, Georgia's gaze zeroed in on Meghan. "And you must be the guest who's living with the pastor."

There was a sudden murmur among those nearby who heard what Georgia had said.

Meghan looked aghast, blanching white in mortification.

"She's *our* guest and is living in the garage apartment, Georgia." Carolyne corrected her loudly enough for those who had overheard Georgia to hear her as well.

Georgia fluttered her fingers as she reached up to feel the pearls around her neck. "Oh, my, yes. I'd heard that. I'm Georgia Bennett," she added, not taking her gaze off Meghan. "And what brings you here?"

"We're here for the Bible study, of course," Carolyne chuckled, though she felt her smile was becoming strained the more Georgia talked. "We're about to find a seat."

"Oh, of course, of course." She didn't move. "Dakota has always opened his house up like some kind of shelter. We pay good donations for a shelter in Dallas, but he insists on bringing the people to his house." Her trilled laughter was meant to make it sound as if she'd meant nothing by her words.

Carolyne knew differently. She wasn't going to let Georgia get away with that, but before she could say anything, Meghan spoke. "And I'm glad he has. I've been in a shelter and hope never to repeat that experience."

Silence fell across the room as those around now strained to hear what was being said.

Georgia puffed up as if she'd been insulted. "And what is the matter with a shelter?"

Meghan flushed. "Nothing, if they're run properly. I, however, landed in one that wasn't. Drugs, sex, booze, it was all there and I was nearly accosted in the process."

"Oh my, oh my." Georgia worried her pearls again. "We'd heard of the alcohol but not the drugs or well…oh my…"

She turned to walk off. Carolyne didn't let her, simply by saying, "Thank goodness she got out of there and came here where she can feel safe."

Georgia was at a loss as to what to say. She had what she wanted—an embarrassed Meghan—and she'd now do her best to spread gossip and get Carolyne's son in hot water. Carolyne could see it in her eyes.

"Well, then, we should find a seat. My, my."

Conversations resumed. But the mood in the study was now different. Some studied Meghan unobtrusively, curious about what Georgia had intimated, while others whispered. Still others showed sympathy in their eyes, as they had been in Georgia's sights at one time or another.

She hoped Meghan would be okay. Carolyne turned to her. "I'm sorry you had to meet the gossipy one first."

Meghan shook her head. "It felt good to be honest about my past."

Carolyne sighed. "She and her husband love to cause problems for Dakota."

Meghan bit her lower lip and then asked, "Is my living in the apartment going to do that?"

Carolyne took Meghan's hand and patted it. "No, honey. God placed you in our path and you shouldn't worry about what a few people may not like."

"You know I wasn't lying. I did try the shelter and it was awful, but if you have one here, and it'll help Cody, I'll be glad to go. I just didn't know where to go, and well…"

Carolyne was already shaking her head. "We don't have a shelter. Cody has brought up the issue many times to the elders but they just don't want to take on the responsibility."

"Well, why don't you open it then?"

Carolyne blinked. "Me?" She'd never thought of such a thing. Open a shelter? In Shenandoah? And run it? "That's crazy…" She hesitated.

"Why is it so crazy?"

Carolyne had already admitted they needed a shelter. "Well, because…" She trailed off. What had been shock at the suggestion by Meghan churned to interest. She discovered that the absurd idea did hold some appeal.

"Or someone. I mean, does it have to be through the church?" Meghan asked.

Ideas formed. The Bennetts loved to control everything and they thought by denying the church the opportunity to open a shelter they would keep the less desirables, as they thought of them, out of town. Of course, no matter what they did, the homeless people were still in town. The Bennetts were of the belief that once out of sight, they were out of mind.

Dakota had a heart for those very people, as did Carolyne. She loved working with people. And she loved creating projects. "I couldn't do it alone," Carolyne murmured to Meghan, not answering her question directly. "I know a bit about business and how to run one from watching my son all these years as he's had to deal with the church. But I'm not as wise on the shelter end."

Meghan snorted. "I could certainly tell you what *not* to do."

Carolyne brightened and glanced at Meghan with fresh hope. "You certainly could."

Meghan's eyes turned wary. "Wait, I didn't mean…"

Carolyne laughed. Grabbing Meghan's hand again, she said, "You told me you wanted to go out and look for a job. Well, what if I have a perfect job for you?" She squeezed Meghan's fingers. "We'll discuss this after the meeting. I think, however, my dear, that you've just found a new ministry for you and me to open together."

Chapter Thirteen

Sarah was happy that it was almost time for her dad to pick her up. He was getting off work early today, and they were going to go shopping for some new clothes for her. She'd been waiting all day for him to pick her up. Their relationship had been strained since Mom died. She sometimes felt her dad blamed her for her mother's death, and then he had moved here without even asking her if she wanted to.

Sarah had been certain her dad hated her—until lately. Lately he had been paying more attention to her, and she got the feeling maybe he didn't hate her so much after all. So, she was in a hurry to finish her homework so she and her dad could spend the day together. She didn't tell him, but it made her really excited that he was going to take her shopping.

Sarah finished her last math problem just as the doorbell rang.

Carolyne opened the door as Sarah started stuffing her books into her book sack. "Hi, Dad!"

Her dad walked in and smiled. "Hey, pumpkin. Clean up your mess and let's go."

She grinned and did just that.

"Carolyne, how are you and Meghan doing today?"

Carolyne smiled. "We need some advice if you have a minute."

Chase nodded, holding his uniform hat in hand. Sarah slowed her packing, wondering what was up. She hadn't done anything.

Her dad crossed to the sofa and took a seat. "So, what's going on?"

"What do you think about a shelter here in town for homeless women and children?"

"Are you asking professionally or personally?"

Meghan cleared her throat, drawing everyone's attention. "Actually, we'd need your opinion on both."

He nodded and set his hat aside. "Professionally I'd have to say the town could certainly use a shelter like that. Of course, there'd be all kinds of permits and such and hoops the person would have to jump through if they were going to open it, and it all depends on where you were going to open it, like in your house or in a public building."

"We'd want to rent a building."

He pursed his lips. "Personally, I'd say the project could be dangerous. Are you two planning to run the shelter by yourself? Are you sure about such an idea?"

"I think it's something we could do," Carolyne argued. "And we'd have to recruit help. But why do you think opening a shelter would be dangerous?"

"If you take in abused women, for instance, you might have to deal with angry husbands. If you take in ex-jailbirds, you might have to deal with whatever baggage they bring with them."

Meghan nodded. "That was the problem in Fort Worth. Anyone could come in, and the people who ran the shelter didn't monitor what went on. They served supper and then locked the doors. There was someone at a desk downstairs, but they never came upstairs."

Carolyne frowned. "Well, I was thinking more of a place for people to come who needed a short stay. We could screen them, find out what's happened, why they're there. And then we could give them a place to shower, a good meal, a bed to sleep in and help them find a job. It wouldn't be for people who weren't willing to work. Everyone there would have to help around the place."

"You've put a lot of thought into this." He shifted his body.

Sarah waited, listening, hoping it was over so they could leave and go shopping. But her dad's next words devastated her.

"Let me see what type of plans you've made."

Sarah waited and waited, her heart starting to hurt all over again as Carolyne, Meghan and her dad brainstormed.

And as it hurt she got angrier and angrier, and she vowed she'd show him how much she hurt. Sarah walked right past them and went outside, and her dad didn't even notice.

It was dark before they left that night. And they never made it shopping.

Three days had passed, and Sarah had done what she had vowed, striking out at her dad.

But now she was scared. Her PE teacher stood in front of her with the principal. Mrs. Patterson was a nice woman but she was all red faced and angry now. She was actually scaring Sarah to death, though Sarah stared back mutinously and refused to answer. If she did, there was no telling what the teacher might do to her friend. And it was her fault because she'd asked Jesse to bring it for her.

"I'll ask you again, where did you get this beer?" the gym echoed with Mrs. Patterson's angry query.

She just couldn't tell on Jesse. She'd wanted to make her father angry, but now she was afraid she might go to jail or worse.

"Did one of the other children give this to you?"

Anger at her dad and at Carolyne and Meghan built up in her. It wasn't fair that they had taken up all of her dad's time and it wasn't fair that her dad was avoiding her again. She felt tears coming to her eyes and fought letting them fall.

"Young lady, answer your teacher," the principal said. Oh yeah, Mr. Zimmerman had to come as soon as he'd heard. He didn't like her. He called her a juvenile delinquent.

"Meghan gave it to me."

She lied. She hadn't meant to, but she'd heard Meghan say something about drinking and stuff going on in the shelter where she'd been. So maybe if she told them Meghan had done it, then they wouldn't punish her so bad. Adults didn't get in as much trouble as kids.

"Which Meghan?" Mrs. Patterson demanded.

Her stomach churned and hurt. She stared at the unopened beer can in the principal's hand. Why hadn't she

kept it in her backpack instead of taking it out and looking at it? She wasn't going to drink it. She'd just wanted
her dad to find it. "She's staying with Ms. Carolyne."

"You're lying," Mrs. Patterson said.

Her stomach clutched. If she was caught lying *and*
with beer, they might send her to kids' jail. She'd heard
about those from Jesse and her dad. Frantically, she
shook her head, needing to make them believe her so
she wouldn't lose her dad completely. "Honest. She
used to drink and do drugs in a shelter in Fort Worth."
Sarah tried to remember what she'd heard Meghan say.
"She lost her job. She was drunk when she came here.
She said she wasn't going to drink anymore and she
didn't need it. So I took it. She threw it out, you know."

"Mrs. Ryder wouldn't allow such things to go on in
her house," the principal informed her.

She shook her head. "That's why Meghan threw the
beer out. She didn't want to make Ms. Carolyne mad.
I'm so sorry. I won't do it again. Just don't call my dad."

"Too late."

Her stomach twisted and acid filled it at the sound
of her father's voice near the door of the gym. The color
drained from Sarah's face.

"Beer?" His voice cracked with incredulity.

"This is very serious, Mr. Sandoval."

That principal just had a way of saying things. She
shook her head. "I wasn't going to drink it."

"She had it in her hands when I came in to make sure
all the girls were out before I locked up for lunch," Mrs.
Patterson informed her father.

"I was just looking at it." Sarah argued but knew
how feeble that excuse sounded.

Her dad snorted and her heart hurt. He didn't believe her. "It's true!" she protested.

"That's enough, young lady," Mr. Zimmerman said. "Go sit over there until I'm done talking with your father."

She stood her ground for a minute but then wilted and did as she was told, going over and plopping down on the bleachers.

Chase watched her go. He was furious.

The principal motioned him outside the gym and Chase followed. When the door shut behind him, he turned to Mr. Zimmerman. "Where did she get the beer?"

"She says from a lady she's staying with."

"Carolyne?" His voice rose and he forced it down. Steam poured out of his ears, or at least it felt that way.

"No, the new lady in town—Meghan."

Chase stumbled back at that.

"I don't believe her though. She told us Meghan was getting rid of the beer and tossed it out. She got it from there."

Chase shook his head. His thoughts were jumbled. He felt as if he'd walked into someone else's life. This couldn't be happening with his daughter. Not again. Things had been starting to turn around until this. "She's lying," he stated flatly.

"The question is, why is she lying? Who is she covering for?" Mr. Zimmerman studied Chase. "Could she have brought the alcohol from home?"

Chase shook his head. "I don't drink—ever. I know I did a few times when I was a kid but that was before I became a Christian and when I was acting out."

"I guess the apple doesn't fall far from the tree then, does it, Mr. Sandoval."

He really wanted to punch the principal for that remark. Chase could tell that Zimmerman had marked Sarah as a bad kid who was never going to change and that made him furious.

"Someone gave it to her," he informed the principal.

"These excuses keep coming up, Mr. Sandoval," Zimmerman answered. He slid his hands into his pockets, causing his suit jacket to bunch up. "I'm not interested in excuses. I'm interested in Sarah."

Chase's anger faded. "So am I."

"You need to discover why she's acting out."

Chase felt like a broken record as he repeated, "Her mother died recently."

Mr. Zimmerman nodded. "I understand that. But Sarah seemed to be changing lately, until today. What is it that keeps triggering her anger? As a parent, I think you really need some counseling on this."

Chase resisted the idea. "What's that going to help?"

Zimmerman frowned. "She's not talking to you, that's obvious from her reaction when she saw you come in. A mediator might help you two work through her grief and open up to each other. She seemed upset and scared when you walked in, which is a good sign. I've seen a lot of kids who didn't care if their parents knew what they did or not. With that in mind, I would really suggest you see someone to try to get to the bottom of why she's doing these things."

He resisted the idea but answered, "I suppose I could make an appointment with Pastor Ryder."

"He does a lot of counseling. That might be a good idea," the principal agreed.

Zimmerman turned to go back into the gym. He called to the teacher and had her come out and then nodded toward the door. Together Zimmerman and Mrs. Patterson left.

Chase took a deep breath and pulled open the door to go into the den of contention.

Sarah sat on the bench in front of the lockers. The locker room wasn't much different than the boys' locker room had been all those years ago. Pale green lockers, stacked double, lined the wall, with four benches the same color sitting in the room on the concrete floor. Showers lined the far wall and a huge bucket for trash sat right by the door.

Sarah had been crying. Though she quickly dashed away the tears, Chase saw the telltale signs in the red-tipped nose and swollen eyes.

He softened, but then forced those feelings away. He couldn't let her think this was acceptable behavior. He rested his left hand on his gun while his right hand gripped his cowboy hat. Crossing over, he sat down on one of the other benches, both to keep from shaking her and to keep from hugging her.

He had never been so angry in his life.

They both sat in silence for a minute before he finally said, "What did you think you were doing? Beer!" His voice rose. "You've only just turned twelve!"

"So what do you care?" she shouted back and started to get up to run out of the locker room.

"Sit back down. Now!"

She plopped down on the bench and crossed her arms over her chest.

"Who gave you that beer? And don't tell me it was Meghan."

Her chin went up in the air.

Okay, though he wanted to know, and was determined to find out, he'd try a different tack. "Do you have any idea what alcohol will do to your brain and your liver? And at your age, if you start drinking, you'll end up in juvenile hall. Not only that, you won't be able to hold down a job, and if you ever get a driver's license, you'll end up in a wreck, either killing yourself or worse, someone else who is innocent. Would you like to hear the statistics?"

He started quoting her the stats but she sat there like a statue.

"What do you have to say for yourself?"

She shrugged. "I didn't mean for the teacher to see it."

Fresh waves of anger swept through him. "I'll bet you didn't. So, tell me, how many other times have you had beer and not been caught?"

Her lower lip trembled and then firmed up. "None," she replied as sarcastically as possible.

He forced himself to sit still and prayed for help to keep from jerking his daughter up and shaking her. *Why is she being this way, God?*

His wife's face floated into his thoughts and his anger faded. She'd done such a good job with Sarah. He was a total failure as a father. She'd started getting into trouble and it seemed no matter what he did, it only got worse.

"Fine then. You're not going to be honest with me. But there's someone I think you'll be honest with. Pastor Ryder."

Her eyes widened and she dropped her arms. She once again looked like his little girl. "Please, Dad. I don't want to tell him."

He thought briefly about giving in. She looked so young and innocent. But so many of the criminals who came into his office looked the same way. He shook his head. "I'm sorry, Sarah. But we're going to go to counseling."

"Counseling!" She jumped up, shock in her voice.

"What did you think I meant?" he asked, bewildered.

"I thought you were going to make me tell him so Meghan would get in trouble."

His mouth thinned. "Oh, you'll tell him, but Meghan isn't going to get in trouble because she didn't give you that can. And then you're going to tell Dakota just why you find it necessary to have beer in the first place, to hang around kids who are causing trouble and why you're lying."

"I don't want to go," she insisted.

He shrugged, feeling very old and very tired. Standing, he said, "You no longer have a choice. I'm not letting you head down the wrong path, Sarah. I don't care to what lengths I have to go. I love you too much."

Her eyes filled with tears even as her face hardened. It hurt him to see that look. "We'll go to Pastor Ryder and you are going to talk to him and we're going to get to the bottom of this, no matter how long it takes."

When she didn't say anything, he turned toward the door. "Come on. You've been suspended from school

for the next three days and I have some chores I want
you to do."

"Chores?"

Chase pushed open the door of the gym. "Oh, yeah.
If you think you are going to have three free days while
you're out of school, think again. The list in my mind
is growing even as I walk. As a matter of fact, I can think
of so many things, you're liable to be busy for the next
month."

Miserably Sarah walked past him as he pulled out his
cell phone to call Dakota and set up a time to talk about
his budding juvenile delinquent.

Chapter Fourteen

The night breeze had turned cooler. No longer were there any leaves on the trees except for the evergreens that dotted some of the front yards along the block. Meghan pushed at the ground, rocked the swing on the front porch and sighed contentedly.

Dakota wasn't home yet. Carolyne and Meghan had shared dinner with each other and now they were on the porch.

Meghan pulled her sweater about her. "I'm going to hate when it gets colder and I can't be outside. The air here is so wonderful."

Carolyne nodded. "It won't be long. The chill makes me think we're going to have a bad winter." Carolyne shifted in her chair and reached for her hot cup of coffee. Turning back to Meghan, she confided, "I have our ideas drawn up and was planning on talking to Dakota tonight—"

She paused and then chuckled when she saw him coming down the street in his compact.

"Guess you can. Should I go in?" Meghan asked as she started to get up.

"No," Carolyne halted her with a shake of her head. "You're part of this. Stay."

Meghan thought it would have been nice for Dakota and his mom to have some time alone, but since Carolyne didn't seem to want it right now, Meghan eased back down into her seat. She was on her cane tonight. Evidently she'd done too much yesterday, because she'd woken up today and found she was having trouble walking again.

As Dakota strolled up, Carolyne asked, "Have you eaten?"

He nodded. "I grabbed a sandwich on the way home."

Glancing at Carolyne, Meghan felt her face heat and was glad it was twilight out. She had no business feeling what she did for this man. He was a friend from aeons ago and it was best kept that way.

"So, what have you two been up to tonight?" He walked up the stairs and took a seat next to his mom, facing Meghan.

Carolyne smiled. "Something that I'd like to discuss with you."

Surprised, Dakota turned toward his mother. "This sounds serious."

"In a way." Carolyne leaned back in the chair and clasped her hands, as was her habit. "Did you know Meghan was in a shelter for a short time in Fort Worth?"

Dakota glanced back at her and sympathy was in his eyes. "I'm sorry to hear that."

She shrugged, embarrassed. Carolyne continued,

however. "She was attacked there and the drug use was rampant."

Dakota started up out of his seat as if to come over to her but his mom stopped him. "She's fine. She wasn't hurt but that just underscores what I'm saying. Can you imagine Meghan, who has done nothing, being hurt in one of those places?"

Dakota found he didn't want to think about it. Meghan nearly raped. His pulse pounded in his ears.

"I want to open a shelter here."

Dakota turned back to his mom, his fear for Meghan pushed aside. "What? But you just said—"

"Exactly, son. We need a good shelter here. Have you seen all the people on the streets? These are hard times for many. And if they can't take a bath, they can't interview for a job. If they're hungry, how can they concentrate on filling out an application? Meghan and I have discussed the idea and she is willing to help me. She had planned to go out and get a job, but she's agreed to live at the shelter full-time and help run it. She needs a job. We need a shelter. And I—this is something I think I've wanted to do for a while though I'm only now realizing it."

"But Mom," Dakota started. His thoughts whirled. Two women in charge of a shelter? That was too dangerous.

"Chase has looked over our initial plans and wants to help as well. He is a great carpenter—remember when he was a teenager? And we'd screen the people we accept in."

"Your mom has been very thorough," Meghan added.

Frustrated, Dakota ran a hand through his hair. "The

church will never go for it. I've tried to open a shelter before."

"We're not going through the church," Meghan said quietly.

His gaze shot to hers and then to his mom's. "Well then, how?"

Carolyne laughed. "You've been a pastor too long, honey. There are other ways of helping the community. And if we start it up, unlike you, we don't have to get the elders' approval."

"But what about finances?" he asked.

"There are grants that we qualify for and I can get a business loan if I have to."

"Where would you put the shelter?"

"One of the empty buildings downtown."

Dakota winced. The Bennetts would love that. But then, on the other hand, he had wanted to see a shelter opened since he'd taken over the church. "You know," Dakota said, thinking of the building he'd wanted to rent for the youth, "if you go through a Realtor other than the one I've been using, the huge building we wanted for the youth would be available, and at a good price."

His mom laughed. "Thank you, honey. I'll show you the plans and tell you what we've been discussing, but first—"

Dakota saw his mother glance behind him toward the neighbors' house.

"—I need to go talk to the sisters." She stood. Leaning down, she kissed her son on the cheek and hurried down the stairs, leaving Dakota with Meghan.

The porch was quiet, the sound of the wind and the occasional car the only noise. He could hear his mom call out to the sisters and the two sisters reply as they started up a conversation.

In the near darkness, he could make out the planes of Meghan's face. She was watching him, her eyes steady and sure. He also noticed the cane by her leg, resting on the chair.

"How are you today?" he asked.

"Good. And you? You look tired."

He shook his head and rubbed the back of his neck. "Been busy as usual. I had several scheduled meetings, as well as a few unscheduled ones. Hospital visits, home visits. Worked on my sermon in between. We broke ground today for the new youth section, and I had to meet with city officials about that, and on the list goes."

She didn't say anything for a long time, and he wondered what she was thinking. The sound of his mom's laughter drifted across the lawn.

"You're trying to do everything yourself."

Her voice was so soft, he almost didn't hear her. When it registered what she'd said, he sat up. "Excuse me?"

"You're tired, Cody." She used his childhood name. "You leave before light many days and get back after dark. You're spreading yourself so thin that you're losing out on so much."

Offended, Dakota smiled tightly and explained, "I'm only doing my job."

Meghan backed off, or so he thought. Her gaze cut to the side. Her hand touched her cane and, just as he was about to apologize for sounding short, her soft voice came back, "Your mom has been researching my disease. I'll never be able to repay her for all she's done for me. I made an appointment with a neurologist, for Monday, and have contacted the National Multiple Sclerosis Society and Multiple Sclerosis Society of America who both had information about how to slow the progress of this disease."

"That's great." Dakota had been worried about Meghan's condition and was glad to know something could be done about it. His mother had explained a bit to him about it and her plans to help Meghan.

"She also found out that if I do too much, it can cause fatigue. You see, yesterday I overdid it and today I'm on the cane because of that."

"Well then," Dakota said, immediately worried, "you'd better slow down and think next time. We want you healthy."

Meghan's gaze lifted to Dakota's. "Your mom wants *you* healthy."

He hadn't seen that trap coming. Consternation filled him. Before he could reply, Meghan continued, "Your mom misses you. She's never said it, but she sets a place for you every night and then takes it away when you don't show up. She's mentioned a couple of times the stress that lack of sleep can cause and that it sends many to an early grave."

"Meghan—"

"Hear me out, please, Dakota. I owe your mother this much. I'm an outsider and can observe what sometimes those close to a situation wouldn't see."

Dakota let out a long sigh and then nodded. Sitting back, he waited for Meghan to continue.

"I really don't mean to pry, but this youth project… You have a full-time youth pastor. I've seen him the few times Carolyne and I have been up to church. He spends a lot of time praying and working on his sermon but little time helping out. Oh, I know he visits the youth and things, but really, why isn't he the one overseeing this youth project? Doesn't he want to or is it because you are always jumping in before he has a chance? He's young and new. Have you wondered if maybe you intimidate him when it comes to certain things?"

She waited and he realized she wanted a response. "He's always asking questions."

She nodded. "Put him in charge of overseeing everything that has to do with the kids. He can bring the plans to you and let you make the final decision, but that would take so much off your shoulders."

He didn't comment but thought about her words. "That would ease my load. But I'm just not sure—"

"You trust him with the youth?"

"Of course I do." He was bothered that she'd ask that.

"Then why not trust him with an inanimate object?"

She had him there. Guilt touched him. "You're right." He hadn't realized he'd been controlling so much of the youth program. Now that Meghan mentioned it, he saw in hindsight that his youth pastor had been wanting to get involved but Dakota had been so busy doing that, he hadn't seen Jeff's desire to help.

"Can I say something else?" she asked timidly.

He grinned. "You might as well."

She clasped her hands much the way his mom did when she was concentrating. "I've been reading in Acts, and it made me wonder why the elders and deacons of the church aren't helping with hospital visits and home visits and other things like that."

"Huh?" He was glad she had been reading in Acts, but what was she talking about?

"You know, Stephen and those who were appointed to take care of the widows?"

He blinked.

"Why aren't the people at this church helping out like that?"

Embarrassed, he had to admit, "We've never done it that way."

"Why not?"

Her innocent question struck a chord in his heart. "I don't know. But you're right. And I do know other churches have people who go out and do things like that. Still, this church isn't used to change."

"They wouldn't let you build a shelter."

He nodded. "Very frustrating." And it had frustrated him to no end that they wouldn't let him start that project. They didn't want change, didn't want that type of people associated with their church. Their church? It was everyone's church. It was God's church.

"And yet, you aren't willing to change and allow others to help?"

Conviction hit him between the eyes. He was angry that others wouldn't change, but here he was leaning toward the same problem. He could handle it because they'd never done it that way before. He hadn't realized he was being just as immovable as some in the church. In utter disbelief he stared at the woman before him. How many years had his mom been suggesting the same things but Meghan was able to turn him inside out and make him see that he was doing too much and not allowing his church to help.

She made him see things that he'd never seen before. Had he been so busy that he wasn't paying attention to God, and God had to send this wonderful woman to shake him up and get his attention?

"What are you thinking about?"

He realized he was still staring at Meghan. He got up, moved over next to her and sat down on the swing. "You."

This close he could smell the soft scent she wore and see that his answer disconcerted her. "I didn't offend you, did I?"

Her golden hair hung in soft strands and he wanted to reach up and touch one. It was quite beautiful with the inside light from the house reflecting through the lace curtains and highlighting the gold in her hair.

"Never," she said as he studied the top of her head. When she didn't look up, he reached down and touched her chin.

He released her chin and sat back a bit to break the spell. "I was thinking that you have been a godsend, Meghan. I've been working so hard that, though others have tried to point out how busy I was, I didn't slow down to hear. In the short time you've been here, you have analyzed my life and pointed out some areas that need changing."

"Oh, I didn't mean to—"

"No." He touched her lip and then pulled his hand back, thinking that was too intimate. "No," he repeated and took her hand. It was small, soft, and trembled. "It just amazes me how accurate you are. Maybe I *have* been too busy and stuck in my own ways to see what you pointed out."

"I wasn't criticizing you," she argued.

Dakota smiled tiredly. "I didn't take it as that, sweet Meghan." Her hand felt so good that he found he didn't want to release it, especially when those tiny fingers of hers curved around his larger hand. He felt peace, something he realized he hadn't felt in a long time.

He leaned back and rested next to her. "You know, I haven't had much time to talk with you, but I find I enjoy it."

Rest filled him and he asked, "What are your plans, Meghan?"

She shifted uncomfortably. "I don't understand."

He squeezed her fingers and reluctantly let go of her hand. "Your plans. What do you see yourself doing for the future?" With a toe, he pushed the swing into motion, causing it to rock back and forth in a soothing, relaxing motion.

Meghan hesitated. He shifted his hands behind his head and stretched out, waiting, allowing his knees to bend with the swing as it moved. "I'm not sure," she answered.

"Well, then, what are they for tomorrow? Talk to me," he encouraged. "Your voice is soothing."

It was, but he also wanted to put her at ease.

It worked.

"Well, I have to learn to pace myself, as your mom said."

He nodded.

"We're going to go to the doctor about medication and see about financial help from the MS Foundation since I don't have insurance. Your mom has really done so much to help me. And of course, she's asked me to help with the shelter."

"So you'll be staying here," Dakota surmised and that thought pleased him. He sat up, sliding his arm behind her on the swing and turning to face her.

He saw surprise on her face. "I guess I am. I hadn't really thought about it, but if I do help your mom, then yes, I suppose I have decided to stay here. But I'll have my own place to live soon at the shelter," she added.

"Don't worry about that, Meghan. This isn't an inquisition. I was just curious about your plans."

"I'll have a job, a place to live…." She trailed off. "I don't know what else."

"What did you do as a job before?" he asked and turned back to face forward. His mother was currently listening to Mary as she expanded on something about the building and undesirables. He couldn't make out the entire conversation—they were too far away.

"I have done some bookkeeping and computer work. Secretarial things."

"That'll be a good help to my mom. She hates that stuff," he told her with a grin in his voice. He felt her relax beside him.

"Thank you for all you've done for me," she whispered.

He shook his head. "Don't thank me. Thank God. He's the One who orchestrated this."

She sighed. "It's still going to take time for me to see God's hand in every area of my life. I mean, I came here looking for you when I was—drunk."

He nodded. "And isn't it amazing that we still live here? And that we just happen to have that extra room? And that your situation has given my mom a purpose?"

"Well, when you put it that way…" He heard the smile in her voice.

"Exactly. God brought a childhood friend to your memory, even though you weren't serving Him, and He led you back here. He has plans for you, Meghan. You just take time, get well, and don't rush it, and you'll find what He has in store for your life."

"You, too," Meghan said pertly.

Dakota laughed. "That's the spirit. I think that is the first time you've spoken to me like that, except for the first day."

Meghan groaned. "Please don't remind me of that."

Dakota laughed. "At least you had some spirit."

"Well if you would come around more often, you might find I have more than you realize." She raised an eyebrow.

Dakota turned, his own eyebrows raised. "Is that so?"

She smiled and he could tell her cheeks had darkened some. He leaned back in the swing, causing it to rock, and laughed.

"What's so funny?" his mom asked, walking up, Mary and Margaret tottering along behind her.

He shook his head. "I think you've been working on the girl. You've changed her when I wasn't looking, Mom."

His mother chuckled. "Not at all. You're just finally meeting the real Meghan."

He glanced at Meghan. "The real Meghan, huh?" His gaze traveled her face, and softly, so that only Meghan could hear, he said, "I find I like the real Meghan."

"So what do you think?"

He realized Mary had been talking to him. And he'd completely missed what she had said. Turning his attention to Mary, he replied, "I think I'm going to relax for a while tonight and sit here and enjoy you ladies' company."

Mary blinked. "Well now, that's grand, but that wasn't what I asked, was it?" She looked to Margaret.

"Hmmph." Margaret made a noise and sat down next to his mom.

Dakota grinned. It was going to be a long, enjoyable night.

Chapter Fifteen

"Just take it slowly." Dakota helped Meghan through the back door. Though he'd arrived early at church as he always did, his mom and Meghan had come later, as was his mom's habit. And, of course, his mom always came in the back door too, so she could then stop by the office and put fresh flowers on his desk before going out front.

Meghan was moving slowly. She sighed. "I don't know why I am having trouble with my leg today." She paused and rubbed the muscle in her left thigh. "I didn't do too much yesterday. It's cramping up in the thigh and sometimes refusing to hold any weight."

Dakota wondered as well. Meghan's leg nearly dragged as she awkwardly used her cane to rest her weight on it. She winced and quickly shifted her weight. She'd chosen a dark blue dress for the Sunday service that tucked in toward the knees. He wondered, though it was a beautiful dress, if it made walking hard.

"Just something else we'll have to research, dear—or ask the doctor when we go to the appointment," Carolyne said.

Meghan nodded. "Every time I think I have this figured out, something changes."

"God is in control," Dakota murmured and turned to walk by her side as they entered the main sanctuary. He rested his hand on her back so he could pace himself. And because he liked touching her.

She glanced up at him in recognition of his actions and then back down to the floor.

The sanctuary was over halfway full. Of course, when the music started at ten and people started singing, he knew he'd see several more families sneak in. During the first half hour of the service, many families would slip in and find seats. And as church neared the end, there were always those who would slip out—some for work, but many because they had "put in their time" and were ready to go hunting or fishing or to visit family for Sunday dinner.

It saddened Dakota in many ways because he believed that church shouldn't be just a social occasion here on earth, it should be about learning and growing and drawing closer to those who would one day be in heaven. Christianity was all about a relationship, but in America, so many saw it only as an obligation. Dakota shook his head and wondered what he wasn't doing right to reach these people.

His mom touched his arm. "Dark thoughts?"

"No. Not really." His attention turned to Meghan as they made their way to the first pew, where his mother always sat. "You okay?"

Meghan nodded and sat down with relief. "I'm sorry about the trouble."

Genuinely surprised, he said, "Meghan. When are you going to realize you're not trouble to me?"

She smiled.

He returned the smile and continued smiling as he looked up to glance around at his friends and acquaintances. His smile stayed fixed as he looked for visitors, but it strained when he saw the Bennetts and some of the other elders glowering at him from the back of the church.

Oh, brother.

He glanced back at Meghan and his mother. "I need to go say hi to the congregation."

"Of course, son." His mom nodded and then returned her attention to Meghan.

Meghan's gaze on his looked a bit panicked but she nodded too. She was nervous, being on the front pew.

Dakota proceeded to go out and greet his friends and buddies, as well as those whom he only saw on Sunday mornings. He enjoyed getting to say hi to everyone, though some mornings he felt rushed in the process. But then he reminded himself of what Meghan had said about him being too busy and forced himself to slow down and talk to those around him—even as he saw Mr. Bennett making his way toward him.

He continued to smile, silently asking God why this man had to do his best to end any joy Dakota felt this morning—for he knew that was Mr. Bennett's plan from the hard look in his eyes.

"Pastor, can I talk with you?"

"Now isn't a good time," Dakota hedged.

Zachary's eyes darkened. "Well, now, I'm worried about that there girl you have sitting on the front pew," Zachary said, ignoring Dakota's words.

Unable to be rude and simply pass by Zachary, Dakota stopped and smiled. "She isn't feeling her best today but I think she'll be fine later."

Mr. Bennett shook his head. "That's not what I meant. It looks unseemly to have that young girl sitting up there by your mom. People might be getting the wrong idea."

He refused to ask what Mr. Bennett meant. He knew well enough, but if he was interested in Meghan, whose business was it?

Interested? He blinked, not realizing when he'd started thinking of Meghan that way. But he did. He realized he wanted to be around her and talk with her and spend time with her. He shook his head. Now was not the time for such a revelation. Not just before the service, and certainly not in front of this man who was studying him so intently.

And who read him so well. "I thought we'd discussed this. Look at her. She's crippled. She can't walk right. She's got that disease her grandma had. She's going to take up all of your time. Are you sure you want to put your church second to her? After all, this is your job—the church."

Dakota felt his temper rising and decided the best thing to do was walk away. "I'm sorry, Zach, but I see a visitor who just came in. I need to go greet him. Excuse me."

Zachary Bennett's face darkened. He wasn't used to being dismissed. Dakota walked past him and noted the other elders in the back, the others who were Zachary's cronies, watching him with disapproval.

Why were they so determined to watch out for Dakota? Of course, he knew the answer to that. They wanted absolute control. How had he allowed this to happen? When had they started controlling his personal life and personal time?

He couldn't afford to be upset at the moment. Asking God to help him control his temper, he made his way to the visitor and struck up a conversation.

The church service went quickly, it seemed, as they sang and had announcements and some special music. And then Dakota delivered his sermon on love. As he talked about the love Jesus had and the true meaning of love—laying down a life for a friend—he couldn't help but find his gaze being repeatedly drawn to Meghan.

She was radiant in that outfit, and looked so good sitting right there by his mom. He was so glad she'd come into his life—or *back* into his life, he thought, though the child he knew wasn't anything like the woman he was getting to know.

When he was done with the sermon, he gave an altar call and prayed with those who wanted prayer. And then the youth pastor prayed dismissal while he went to the back of the church.

Dakota chatted with each person as they left, listening to their joys and their problems. Many made comments about his sermon or wanted to chat about hunting. Dakota preferred fishing, really.

The Bennetts stood around, waiting to talk with him, but when they realized he was intent on not being drawn out, they left. Oh, they wouldn't do anything where others could hear. And he knew they weren't done with the subject. But, he also knew that as soon as something else new came along, they'd drop it. After all, they couldn't control his private life. Not really.

He shook his head.

After nearly forty-five minutes, everyone was gone except Dakota, and so he finally locked up and drove home. His mom had lunch on the table when he came in.

"Roast, my favorite." Dakota slipped off his jacket. He unbuttoned his cuffs and folded up his sleeves before washing his hands in the sink.

"And mashed potatoes, carrots and gravy." Carolyne set the gravy on the table.

Meghan seated herself. Dakota noticed. "You seem to be walking better."

She shook her head. "I don't understand it. I think it may be that spasticity that the printouts talked about."

"What?" Dakota asked.

His mom explained. "The muscle will contract and not release because it's not getting the neural signal. We discussed it on the way home. Her muscle is relaxed now and she's getting around better."

All seated at the table, Dakota blessed the food. When he was done, he said, "Well, you'll find out at your doctor's appointment tomorrow. And I hope you keep me informed."

"We will, dear," his mom said to him and he grinned at Meghan. Seeing the returning smile, he said, "How about after lunch we go fishing?"

Carolyne laughed. "When was the last time you went fishing, Dakota?"

He chuckled. "It's been too long."

"I've never been fishing," Meghan confessed.

"That settles it! There's no Sunday-night service tonight, and so I'm going to take you two ladies out to our famous fishing hole."

Carolyne frowned. "Meghan, are you up to it?"

"I think so. If I don't overdo it, I mean."

"Great then." Dakota dug into his lunch.

Meghan, he noted, ate her lunch quickly as well. She seemed to be looking forward to the trip as much as he was.

As soon as he was done, he excused himself and changed clothes. When he returned to the living room, he found Meghan also in jeans and a long-sleeved top. His mom was wearing a pair of old khaki pants, a button-up short-sleeve top with a sweater—and a crazy gardening hat.

"To keep the sun out of my eyes," she said and everyone laughed.

They loaded into the car and in fifteen minutes were at the fishing hole.

"So what do we do?" Meghan asked immediately upon exiting the car.

"Well, I'm going to read," Carolyne informed them. She opened the trunk and pulled out a folding chair. Meghan watched as she crossed to a nearby evergreen and set up the chair. Taking her seat, she pulled a book out of her purse and began to read.

"I thought we were going fishing," Meghan said.

Dakota chuckled. "That is how my mom fishes. Come on, you can fish with me."

Reaching in, he pulled out a tackle box and two fishing poles. He handed them to Meghan and then grabbed the two other chairs he'd packed. "Follow me." Dakota walked slowly enough to make sure Meghan had no trouble following him.

At the edge of the water he set up the chairs and took the poles from her.

Meghan sat down, and then Dakota sat down next to her and laid the poles aside. Opening the box, he pointed out what was inside. "It's been so long, but I still have my lures. Worms, fish, flies."

"That one's pretty." Meghan pointed to a silver, metal fish.

He grinned. "Okay." He lifted the line on her pole and attached the lure.

He chose a different one for his pole and then closed the box. "I usually stand up, but we can sit today. Do you know how to cast?"

Meghan shook her head.

"Well, then, we're going to have to stand to teach you."

Meghan stood up, and it was funny to watch her hold the pole out in front of her with both hands.

This was going to take some time. He laid aside his own pole and walked over to her. "The first lesson is to relax."

"I'm worried that the hook is going to hook me," she said and Dakota chuckled.

"I've had that happen once or twice, that's true. But it doesn't hurt. What does hurt is if you step on it or jam it into your hand, which you won't do if you are careful."

"What about my hair?" She reached up and touched it.

Dakota reached up and brushed it back. The curly and silky strands flowed over his hand. "That shouldn't be a problem. Let me show you."

He stepped behind her. "Pick a place out there where you want to cast your line. Right there," he said, pointing. "Now...wait!"

She lifted the pole straight up as if to throw it over her head. "To the side." He grabbed her arms from behind. That brought her flush up against him. He suddenly felt protective of her, and an odd urge to pull her closer. He liked having her here. Reluctantly, however, he moved slightly to the side. "Take the pole here, to the right like this, and when you have it back even, give it a good flick of the wrist. When you do, you have to hold down here—" he indicated the handle "—and the line will go flying."

On the first try the lure fell at her feet. "Oh dear!"

"You just need to flick your wrist and arm a bit harder." He stepped from behind her. "Watch me with my pole."

He picked up his pole and cast out his line. The whirring was loud as the line sailed through the air and landed with a plop in the water.

"You make it look so easy," she muttered.

He chuckled as he reeled in the line. "You try with yours."

She did and her line landed at the edge of the water, making a tiny ripple that spread outward. "Good. Reel it in and try again."

He cast his line out again and smiled as he wound it back.

"Don't you leave it out for the fish to bite?" she asked curiously, watching him.

He nodded, his eyes meeting hers briefly. "I just want you to get used to casting your line first and then we'll tease the fish."

"Tease them?"

He chuckled. "First lesson first. Cast again."

He cast his own line and thought how wonderful it was to hear the whir and plop that spoke of relaxation.

Meghan reeled her line in and turned to the side again to cast it. Dakota observed her posture.

"Your arm is going too far back. You won't have as much control." He debated whether to go over and give her another lesson. He liked having Meghan in his arms and guiltily found that he was looking for another excuse to do just that.

"Like this?" she asked.

Before he could answer, he felt a stinging in his scalp. Then pain.

"Yow!" He jerked and felt his scalp tear.

"Oh no!" Meghan gasped beside him.

"My head!" He grabbed and sure enough, Meghan's hook had found a mark.

She dropped her pole. "Oh oh no!" she repeated and reached for his head.

His breath hissed as her pole bounced on the ground and pulled the hook out. His own pole hit the ground.

He dropped to his chair.

"I'm so sorry." Meghan reached for his head, trying to find the wound.

"Don't worry, Meghan." He shook his head then winced, his eyes squeezing shut as he felt around the top of his head. When Meghan's hands touched his head to examine it, he suddenly found he didn't mind the pain. Her hands felt good. "That was…ouch…what I meant…ouch…about tossing your line too far back. And then I was standing too close—" He didn't open his eyes but relaxed and let her run her fingers through his hair.

"Are you okay, honey?" Carolyne called.

His eyes snapped opened as he remembered that his mom was there. "Yeah, Mom." He heard her approaching through the crunch of leaves.

"I'm so sorry, Carolyne." Meghan's voice reeked with self-recrimination.

He felt his mom's hands and flushed. He hadn't minded Meghan examining him, but now he was starting to feel like a kid. "Really, Mom. It's only a scratch."

He looked up into the knowing eyes of his mother and grimaced again. She had that know-it-all smile of hers that said she knew exactly what he was thinking. How did she *know?*

"I'll go back to reading then. You kids have fun."

She wandered off, leaving him in the chair with Meghan fretting beside him.

"I don't know if I want to fish anymore," Meghan told him worriedly.

"To borrow a phrase from our dear neighbors—Nonsense. Accidents happen."

"I could have hooked an eye," Meghan exclaimed. She twisted her hands together in worry.

Dakota rubbed his head. "It just means you need a bit more practice."

He stood and moved up to her side. He had to admit he was glad his mom had walked back over to the small grove of trees. He was intent on Meghan now and wanted to be alone with her. Catching her hands to still them, he said, "It's like riding a bike. You fall off, you get back on, so come on, let's fish." He rubbed his thumbs over the tops of her hands. Her gaze met his and all argument faded.

He released her hands and bent to pick up the pole, still not breaking eye contact. Holding it out, he waited and watched. There was more than fishing going on now—at least where fish were concerned. He watched every nuance of her reaction and realized she was doing the same. The air was no longer chilly but warm and filled with expectation.

He found he liked being here with her and felt as if this was where he should have always been—by her side, together, doing things like this.

She, finally, with great care, accepted the pole.

"Good girl." He smiled.

She scowled at him. "Don't be patronizing."

"Am I?" he asked innocently.

She chuckled and her eyes sparkled. "If you aren't nice, I might just hook you again."

His eyes darkened as her words took on an entirely different meaning to him. "I think it's too late to worry about that."

Curiously, she tilted her head in query and studied his face.

He continued, "You've already hooked me for good."

Realizing what he meant, she dropped her gaze, her lashes hiding her reaction.

The sound of the occasional car zooming past on the nearby highway, dotted with the singing birds and the ever-constant wind, faded as Dakota stepped forward.

He rested his hand over hers where she gripped the fishing pole. "Are you hooked, too, Meghan?"

She, at length, lifted her gaze to his. Her eyes held vulnerability and longing.

Dakota continued, "Because, if you aren't, I plan to keep casting my line until I land you."

"Dakota," she began. Her lips trembled as she hesitated.

He decided he'd said enough. Leaning forward, inch by inch, so she could object if she didn't want him to, he waited until his lips were a breath from hers. "And I *am* going to catch you eventually, Meghan O'Halleran."

His lips touched hers. It was gentle, a taste of promise as they caressed hers. And then finally her lips softened and returned the kiss.

He leaned in and deepened it before pulling back.

The sounds of cars, along with the birdsong were still there, but as far as he was concerned, the entire world had just changed.

It was no longer quite as dull, empty or busy because he had Meghan in it. And more than just having Meghan in it, he realized something more. He was in love with Meghan O'Halleran and could easily spend the rest of his life with her.

In her eyes confusion warred with fulfillment.

He saw it and felt a slight twinge of guilt. He could wait, he realized, while she solved the war raging in her. So, quietly, gently, he said, "But we'll take this at your pace, sweet Meghan."

Then he turned back to the pond. "Now, let's go back to lesson two, casting your line." They spent the rest of the day doing just that.

Chapter Sixteen

Meghan sat restlessly at Dr. Viglio's office. Nervously she crossed her legs and clutched her purse. She hated doctors.

"It'll be okay, honey," Carolyne said from beside her. She set the magazine aside and reached for Meghan's hand. "Trust God."

Meghan nodded. "I'm trying."

But it was more than the appointment that had Meghan squirming. She still couldn't get over the kiss from yesterday. Every time she thought about it, her lips tingled.

When she'd found out she had MS, she had vowed not to love anyone. She couldn't. She was afraid that she would end up destroying everyone around her, just like her grandmother had. Embittered and angry, her grandmother had done her dead-level best to make sure no one else survived her anger. And now the church was angry that Dakota was spending so much time away from them.

She was terrified of that and yet, what had everyone been telling her? Trust God. He is in control.

Could she do that?

"Ms. O'Halleran?"

Meghan glanced up. A nurse in white stood at the door, a chart in her hand. Turning to Carolyne, Meghan asked, "Would you mind coming with me?"

"Of course not." Carolyne stood.

Meghan stood as well. Silently, she followed the nurse back into the room, pausing to be weighed—she had gained one pound—and get her blood pressure taken—it was a bit low.

In the room, she seated herself on the table and waited. Memories of the last time she was in such a room flooded her.

"Are you okay, dear?" Carolyne asked. She sat down in a nearby chair and studied Meghan.

"Last time..." She shuddered. "I only remember being told I had to have tests and then going to them. The pinging and grinding of the MRI, the needle in my spine, the tubes of blood..." She shook her head. "And then I was brought back into a room like this and the nurse wouldn't tell me what was going on—she told me it could be anything and not to worry, that the doctor would talk to me."

How she remembered that visit. It rang in her mind again and again. The utter fear when the nurse had said it could be *anything.* Anything! Cancer? Was she dying? Whom would she tell? Who would care?

In that split moment her life had boiled down to utter terror. Who would miss her if she died?

No one.

Her friends at work? They weren't real friends, not

the type that you confided in. Their main goal in life was to climb the corporate ladder.

Family?

She had no family.

She was utterly, completely, alone and sitting in a room just like this, awaiting horrible news.

But she'd had no idea just how horrible that news was going to be.

"Hello, Meghan. I'm Dr. Viglio."

Meghan was jerked out of the past by the friendly voice of the man who had just entered.

Short, no bigger than Carolyne's five foot one inch, he had a broad smile and gentle eyes.

She felt immediately at ease, or as at ease as she could be inside a doctor's office. She shook his hand. He shook Carolyne's hand, as well.

"So you have multiple sclerosis." He opened her chart to read.

Meghan shrugged.

"Well, that's what it says here. By the way, I took the liberty of calling the last doctor who saw you and got a verbal report."

He pulled up a small round rolling chair and sat down. The nurse stood silently behind him, like a toy soldier, at his beck and call.

He dropped the chart on the counter and then rested his hands on his knees. "So tell me, how do you feel about that?"

She blinked. He couldn't be serious.

When he didn't say anything, she realized he was. "How do I feel?" She laughed nervously. What could she say? "Scared."

He only nodded.

What did he want from her? "Upset," she added.

When he didn't say anything, she frowned. "Angry."

He nodded again. "Sounds normal to me."

Her face flushed. "What do you mean *normal?* I have a terrible disease that will probably put me in a wheelchair. That is *not* normal. I mean, I don't want to believe that, but I *know* that's what happens!"

Her eyes widened and she realized she had just yelled at this nice old man.

He smiled. "Why do you think that?"

She looked from him to the nurse and back. "Well…it's true. That's what happens to people with MS."

The doctor's eyes twinkled and he glanced sideways up at his nurse. "Is that what happened to you, Darlene?"

The nurse shook her head.

She looked from Darlene to the doctor and back. "I don't understand."

Darlene smiled. "Sweetie, I've had multiple sclerosis for fifteen years now."

Meghan studied the woman. She stood straight next to the doctor, her smile at the same time both gentle and understanding. Meghan felt tears burn her eyes. "But you look—normal," she finished weakly. "You can't have MS."

The nurse moved to sit down next to the doctor on another stool. "Define *normal* for me."

Meghan felt as if she was on a ride that was out of control. This was surreal. What was going on? "You're standing, without a cane, walking, smiling…"

Darlene nodded. "That I am. But I've been hospital-ized twice with some severe attacks and used a walker for about a month once during one of those attacks. I sit more than I stand. However, I still hold down a job, still do many things myself, though I don't give shots any-more."

The doctor chuckled. "Her right hand has some weakness in it and I suggested she let the newer girls do the injections."

Meghan shook her head. The first strange ray of hope touched her heart.

"Who have you known, Meghan, that had MS?"

"My grandmother," Meghan whispered.

The doctor's smile faded. Gravely, he nodded. "That was a long time ago, wasn't it?"

Mutely, she acknowledged that he was right.

"Twenty years ago, even ten years ago, research hadn't made the strides it has today. Most people within five to ten years went from the type of MS you have, which is called relapsing-remitting, into secondary pro-gressive. Many ended up in wheelchairs and a few were bedridden. I'm not belittling the severity of MS, but did you know that MS is the most common neurological disorder among women your age?"

She shook her head.

"And we have all kinds of drugs that can slow the ef-fects of the disease. Darlene has been on two different drugs. She is going into her sixteenth year now and you see how well she's doing."

Meghan felt the tears release and trickle down her cheeks. The ray of hope blossomed.

"I won't lie to you, Meghan. No one knows which

way the disease is going to go in each individual. A rule of thumb is to watch the first five years of your disease to get an idea of how severe it's going to be. My rule is, just live each day to the fullest, following one simple rule. If you feel like doing it, go for it, otherwise rest."

He pulled out a small hammer and stood. "I'm going to test your reflexes, have you walk for me, and judge just where you are on the disability scale. Then we're going to test your memory and talk about medication."

Meghan could only nod.

She glanced over at Carolyne and saw Carolyne beaming with excitement.

"Do you think I could work in a shelter?"

The doctor tested one knee and then her ankle before moving to the next one. "I don't know. Do you like that type of work?"

She couldn't take in all he was saying. "I want to help Carolyne when she opens one."

He shrugged as he pulled out a pin. "I'm going to touch you on different areas of your arms and legs. Nod when you feel it."

She nodded each time he poked her.

"Now stand up and I'll show you what I want you to do when you walk."

She stood. "What about fatigue?" she asked as she did as he told her. She found she stumbled once and was a bit off balance, but other than that, she did well, she thought.

"That's the most common symptom. Take it easy when you feel tired. And don't get overheated. Heat really bothers most patients. We also have some different medications that can help that."

She nodded. She did get overheated sometimes. But medicines to help it?

He took her elbow and helped her back over to the table. "You're actually doing very well. Right now I'd say you only have a minor disability. We want to keep it that way."

He handed her a pamphlet he'd filled out that was entitled *EDSS, The Scale of Disability* and then wrote some information in the chart.

"I'm going to send you home with some more pamphlets on the medications. I want you to read them, and we'll contact some different places about getting these meds paid for. We'll get in touch with you as soon as we hear something. But I really think you should consider one of the four medications listed in these pamphlets. Make an appointment, and we'll see you in a week."

"Thank you, Doctor," she whispered, her voice hoarse. "Can I ask you one more thing?"

He paused. "Of course. And if you leave here and have questions, you can always call me. So, what is it you want to ask?"

Meghan wanted to make sure she understood the doctor. "So you don't think this disease will affect my emotions and cause me to—change—do you?"

The doctor frowned. "That's actually a very good question, Meghan. In some cases, the disease can affect your emotions. Many MS patients go on antidepressants because some of these meds will cause depression. Some have to go on them because of the parts of the brain the MS affects. And some simply can't handle the prognosis and retreat from reality and need help coping. But there are others who are never affected that way and never have emotional problems."

Relief flooded her. It meant she wouldn't necessarily be like her grandmother after all.

Fresh tears filled her eyes. "Thank you."

He nodded. "Check out up front," he said kindly and was gone.

The nurse handed her some tissues and then exited the room. Meghan covered her eyes with a tissue as fresh tears fell.

She heard Carolyne get up and come over to her. Carolyne's arms slipped around her. And she just held her.

Meghan whispered, "In some ways I feel like I've received a fresh lease on life." She laughed and then shuddered.

"In many ways you have, sweetheart. I remember your grandmother, and I know how afraid you were you'd turn out like her. But your grandmother wasn't a Christian, Meghan. She didn't have hope like you do. You don't have to face another empty, lonely day, because you know there is Someone there to face it with you."

Meghan nodded. She sat back and wiped her eyes. "I think that has already helped me so much. God, I mean. Knowing that He cares. I don't understand why this has happened though."

Carolyne shrugged. "Sometimes God has to get us down on our backs for us to look up. You found Him because of this disease."

Meghan blinked. "I did, didn't I?"

Carolyne nodded. "And you never know, God might just heal you or this disease could go into remission and you won't have another attack for years."

She nodded.

"But even if it doesn't," Carolyne continued, "and you do end up in a wheelchair like your grandmother, you still have that joy that you found when you gave your heart to Jesus Christ."

Meghan felt the last fears of her former life fade as she accepted the simple truth. Peace flooded her. "It doesn't really matter, does it? Life is short, but eternity is forever."

"Exactly," Carolyne whispered. "We know you won't have this disease forever, just for a short time here."

Meghan hadn't thought of that before. Joy bubbled up in her. For the first time in her life, she was glad she'd gone to the doctor.

She slipped down from the table. "And look at Darlene," she said as they exited the room. "Fifteen years. Hope, Carolyne. There is hope."

"There is always hope in Jesus Christ," Carolyne replied.

Meghan slipped her hand into Carolyne's and squeezed. "Thanks for coming with me today."

"Anytime, sweetheart. Now, I have a question for you."

Meghan accepted the receipt and appointment date card from the receptionist and started for the door. "What is that?" she asked as they left and headed down the hall together.

"How do you feel about my son?"

Chapter Seventeen

How did she feel about Dakota?

For three weeks now she'd wrestled with that question.

She'd felt like an imbecile when she'd answered that she didn't know.

Of course she knew.

Didn't she?

He was a friend.

But more. So much more.

Yet she had MS and he was a pastor who was needed by many. She'd seen it over the past weeks. They were always there, calling, dropping by, needing to talk. And she was needy as well, in the physical way, though lately she had been feeling so much better.

They'd started her on medication. She'd been able to get a special grant from one of the companies the doctor had researched. And when she got a job at the center, she'd be able to pay for her portion of it. Despite Carolyne's protests, she'd gone out and applied for several other temporary jobs. She had an interview in a few days. She was nervous, but happy. Of course, it was only a temporary job, part-time at the health department, but they said they understood about her adjusting to MS. She hoped she got the job.

She had to take shots three times a week, and she was on her second week now. Boy, was that something. Thank goodness Carolyne had been there to help her learn to give herself injections. They wouldn't interfere with a new job as she took them at night.

Meghan took up so much of the Ryders' time at the house lately that she was afraid she was taking Dakota away from his job, but she had to admit, he'd slowed down. He was home every evening before the sun set, and at least three times, even four times, a week he made supper.

Carolyne was happy to see him at home, but she herself wasn't at home as much.

They'd contacted Timothy Letterbed, the new Realtor, and within a week, he had struck an excellent deal for the downtown property that Carolyne wanted to use to open up the shelter. Their grant had come through and they had the money to start the shelter. It was all falling into place so quickly.

Carolyne had been working like mad, getting things going, organizing help and refurbishing the basics to bring the place up to code. And Chase had been there every step of the way. He spent all of his time off working on the building.

Which worried Meghan.

Sarah was always at the Ryder house and she was so

withdrawn. Meghan was worried about her. The young girl had found a place in her heart.

Tonight, they were having a party to benefit the shelter. As Carolyne said, you had to do things like this constantly to keep people involved, or when it came crunch time, they wouldn't have the money. As it looked right now, they'd have enough to pay five steady employees for the next year, plus enough to benefit thirty people, but Carolyne wanted to make sure they had extra money in case of emergencies.

Their party had nearly been stopped by the Bennetts and the Hamptons. Meghan couldn't understand the desire of those people to control everything, but she was quickly learning you didn't cross them.

They didn't like her. That much was obvious from when they'd called to talk with the pastor and she'd answered the phone.

Dakota certainly hadn't appreciated their interrogation of her and had apologized afterward. But it had blown over. And now they were at the benefit—Chase and Sarah, Carolyne, Dakota, Meghan and over half the town, including Mary and Margaret who were running the cakewalk.

A Christian band was currently playing music and booths were set up, selling different crafts, with all the proceeds going to the shelter.

Meghan pulled her sweater closer around her and once again asked herself, just what did she feel for Dakota Ryder?

"And what has you so entrenched in thought tonight, sweet Meghan?"

Meghan jerked as the very person of her thoughts

came up to her. She smiled and debated on what to tell him, finally deciding to tell him the truth. "You."

People jostled Dakota, bumping him into her. He reached out and caught her arms, nodding his acceptance to the person who called out an apology.

Holding on to one arm, he escorted Meghan out of the line of traffic. "That sounds intriguing."

She shook her head and decided to change the subject. "Your mom is excited that you've been home so much more."

They strolled along past the booths, watching as some of the residents looked over the crafts while others played games and still others bought food. "How do you feel about my being home more?"

Meghan blushed. But she had to admit the truth. "I like it, too." But at the same time she didn't. It was wonderful having him there for dinner. They had caught up on years of being separated and learned so many things about each other.

And every night they sat out on the porch, Dakota always by her on the swing, rocking as they chatted. Or, if Carolyne wasn't there, sometimes they simply sat in silence. And that was the problem. They were getting to know each other and becoming too comfortable in each other's presence. Meghan found she loved talking with Dakota, and her mind couldn't seem to forget the kiss they'd shared. The memory was there constantly when he was around and when he was absent. She longed for another such embrace. Unfortunately—why she admitted she didn't like him being around—she was afraid.

Though it was chilly at nights now, she didn't want

to give up their time, but she wasn't willing to face her fear, either. A dilemma.

"I'm glad to hear that." Dakota slipped his hand to the small of her back. That was the first time he'd done something so public—except for the kiss.

Through Carolyne she'd found out that Dakota had heard from someone on the board about his public display of affection and they were angry.

Dakota never mentioned it to her.

"The fund-raiser is going well," Meghan observed.

"In no small part thanks to Chase and Jerry and the others who helped set it up."

"Speaking of Chase," Meghan began.

Dakota glanced down at her and with a twinkle in his eyes, he asked, "Do I have competition?"

Her cheeks turned bright red and Dakota laughed. He pulled her to him and hugged her.

"Will you stop it," she whispered. "Be serious."

His smile still in place, he said, not the least bit seriously, "Okay. This is me being serious."

She shook her head. "I am worried about Sarah."

Dakota's smile faded and he did turn solemn then. "She's going through a hard time after losing her mom. They've been coming in for counseling. I can't say anything more than that. But I fear things are going to come to a head soon. She won't tell us what else is bothering her. But there's something else."

Meghan nodded. "She mentioned to me that her daddy let her put some of her mom's things out the other day."

"Good," Dakota said. "I suggested to Chase that might help Sarah with the adjustment. He'd packed everything up and it was killing him to unpack it. Maybe the two of them unpacking those things will help Chase heal as well."

"I noticed they're coming to church."

Dakota nodded. "Chase is searching for healing. No one expects to have their life turned upside down like that. All I can do is pray for him and be there."

"You think that's why he's thrown himself into this project so much? Because he's still hurting?"

They sidestepped a small child who ran past and then Dakota continued, "I think that's part of it. And of course, my mom can be a healing balm to those who are hurting."

"She's changed my life," Meghan agreed. "You know, I've fallen in love with her and don't think I could move away," Meghan whispered.

They came to the cakewalk and Dakota paused. Turning to her, he asked, "And what about me? Do you think you could leave me?"

"Oh, look, sister! Two more people. That will complete the cakewalk." Mary clapped her hands in delight, her blue hair specially styled tonight for the event.

"Well, come on," Margaret ordered. "Pay up and get in. We're getting ready to start the music, Pastor Cody."

Dakota grinned at Meghan. "Saved by the sisters, but I'll want that answer later."

Meghan swallowed.

Dakota pulled out his wallet and paid the small entrance fee.

"Now, dear, do you think you can walk? I notice you didn't bring your cane." Mary tsked.

"She doesn't always need it, she says, sister," Margaret argued. "She can do it. Pastor Cody will take care of her if she can't."

Mary smiled. "Oh. Yes, of course."

Meghan groaned because everyone was watching with interest as the two sisters talked. "Are we ready to start?" Meghan tried to distract the sisters from her personal life.

They were wonderful women, but they had decided the two were a couple and didn't care who knew it.

"We're just waiting on you to take a place." Margaret moved over toward the CD player. "Now, what we'll do is a lot like musical chairs."

Mary smiled. "Like when you were children. Oh, those were fun days."

"I'm telling them, sister." She frowned at Mary who looked highly offended. "Go around the chairs. When the music stops, grab a chair. The last one with a chair wins a cake. And we have some good cakes here."

"I even baked one," Mary added proudly to Dakota. "Your favorite. Mississippi Mud."

Meghan grinned. Each week they came up with a new favorite that Dakota just loved. They were so happy to have him coming home that they were constantly baking surprises for him.

"Nonsense. His favorite will be my Red Velvet."

"I might not win," Dakota cautioned sagely.

Mary giggled like a schoolgirl. Margaret harrumphed and put the music on.

Meghan and Dakota, along with six other people, started marching around the chairs.

"Are you okay doing this?" Dakota asked as they marched.

She opened her mouth to answer, when the music stopped. She gasped and after a hesitation dived into a chair. Her eyes widened. "Oh boy." She covered her heart. "I'd forgotten how silly this game is."

Everyone was laughing. The person left out threw up his hands. "I want that Red Velvet. Don't no one else claim it!" And he stepped out of the way.

Meghan laughed. She and Dakota both stood and watched as Mary took out one of the chairs and meticulously rearranged the two nearest ones. "It looks like I'm going to be okay. My legs are tired, but I think that's just going to be a fact of life."

He nodded. The music started again. And they started marching.

People stood around laughing and pointing, calling out to family members. It was a fun time. "So, are you ready to answer my question?" he asked when the music stopped.

Everyone dashed for a chair. Meghan overbalanced and fell into one, but managed to keep from falling out.

His question didn't help her. She glared at him. "You did that on purpose."

Eyes wide, he lifted his hands. "Would I do that?"

"You want that cake, don't you?"

He burst out laughing.

A teenager was left out and wandered over to the side to watch and wait and see who would win. They all stood back up, the six of them. Jerry was one of them. He pulled at his pants and adjusted his belt. "Get ready, folks," the sheriff said and they laughed.

The music started back up. Twice more they went around, watching people get disqualified before Dakota was near enough to talk again.

"You aren't answering my question," Dakota accused as they marched once again around the ever-shrinking circle.

She glanced back over her shoulder. "That's right. And I may not, either, if you win."

He stumbled in surprise. "Hey, that's blackmail!"

The music stopped.

They dived for chairs and Dakota and Jerry hit the chair at the same time. Jerry went flying and landed on the concrete ground of the parking lot.

The crowd roared with laughter.

"See if I show up Sunday morning, son," Jerry called out as he climbed to his feet.

Hoots of encouragement came from the crowd watching. Dakota grinned. "I have eyewitnesses. That was a win, fair and square."

They stood while the chairs were rearranged.

Meghan laughed. She was having the time of her life. "I haven't felt this young in years," she confided to Dakota as the music started again.

"It's good to stay young. Just look over at the sisters," he said, and pointed.

Mary was clapping in time to the music, dancing as she did, and Margaret was intent on the CD, even though a ghost of a smile kept turning her lips up occasionally.

The music stopped and Meghan found herself in a chair next to Dakota.

The other person stepped out. They both stood and Dakota smiled. "Just down to you and me it seems."

The crowd chuckled. "Take him out, sister," someone called to Meghan.

"Come on, Pastor, you can do it!" another person shouted.

"Competitive, aren't they?" Meghan observed nervously.

"You guys should get in here and try it," Dakota called back, eliciting a fresh wave of laughter.

Mary took them by the arms and led them out to a white line that the original chairs had sat on. "You two have to stay on this line. Away from the chair. We always do this with the last ones. It gives both of you a fair chance."

Meghan groaned. They were a good five feet from the chair.

Dakota laughed. "Looks like I'm going to get to pick a cake."

"No chance," Meghan argued, though she wasn't sure.

The music started and they marched and marched and marched. It was funny to watch the two of them hugging the line, their eyes intent on the chair.

And just as Meghan was certain the music would never stop, she suddenly realized it had.

With a mad dash, she rushed headlong for the chair. Dakota was on the opposite side and sprinted as well.

Two bodies slammed into each other.

She went flying until two arms caught her and pulled her back—right on top of his lap.

Meghan realized Dakota had rescued her from falling. She looked up into his laughing eyes. "Who won?"

Quietly, so the roaring crowd wouldn't hear, he answered, "We both win, if you answer me yes."

Meghan swallowed. What did he mean? Looking into those eyes full of emotion, she realized she no longer had any questions about how she felt. Why hadn't she realized it before? Why hadn't she seen it? Maybe because she'd been so worried about her MS. But with the freedom of realizing she wasn't going to be like her grandmother came another freedom—the freedom to love. And she did. She loved this man. Very much.

But did she have the right to love him?

"Hey, who won?" someone in the crowd called out, breaking the spell.

Meghan pushed back and stood awkwardly, her cheeks once again red as people called out suggestions to the pastor of what to do with her—all clean suggestions but centering on her just the same.

Margaret waved her hand. "This is very difficult, but I just can't decide who was in that chair first—"

"So they both win." Mary clapped.

The crowd roared.

Meghan blushed.

"Now, which of those cakes are you going to choose, Pastor Cody?" Margaret demanded.

There were about twenty cakes left, but as far as Margaret was concerned, there were only two, the two she and Mary had made.

Meghan realized the two women were in contest for Dakota's affection over their baking, so to distract the people from her and Dakota and stop a feud from erupting, she stepped forward. "I just have to have the Mississippi Mud, if you don't mind. Of all the cakes here, that looks like the best one—and I can attest that it tastes great."

Mary beamed. "Why, dear. I didn't know that was your favorite cake."

Dakota leaned in. "You'd make a good pastor's wife, sweet Meghan."

Meghan nearly fell over.

Had he said what she thought? Of course he had. She watched him collect the Red Velvet cake and walk off.

Marriage?

Had he meant that? Or had he been joking. Surely he'd been joking.

She, of course, knew he enjoyed dating her and wanted to spend time with her—but he didn't have time for a wife—not one who took up as much time as she did, did he?

"Meghan?"

She realized Mary had spoken to her. "I don't think you can cook anything that doesn't taste great," Meghan told the old woman.

On impulse she leaned down and hugged the woman.

When she released her, she saw tears in Mary's eyes. And love.

Meghan stepped back.

"Go have fun," Mary said. "We'll put the cake under the table for you until later, okay, dear?"

Meghan nodded and left, realizing she had many many things to consider over the next few days.

Chapter Eighteen

Sarah didn't want to be here. She hated these after-school meetings that her father had started. Why couldn't he just spend time with her instead of making her air her feelings in front of someone else?

She didn't want to tell someone else how she felt. She wanted her dad to know.

Pastor Ryder walked in and held out his hand to her dad. "Heya, Chase."

He smiled and her father smiled back. His father wore his uniform right now, but that'd change soon. He'd soon be in his jeans and flannel shirt and leave to work on the shelter—the shelter that was going to open in just a few weeks.

And then she'd probably never see her dad again. Pastor Ryder offered his hand to Sarah. She took it. It was warm and dry and he shook her hand as if he really cared.

But he was a friend of her dad's.

"Hello, Sarah."

"'Lo," she mumbled. Seeing the look her dad shot her, she sat up straighter. "Pastor Ryder," she added politely.

Her dad nodded.

"So, how have you been this week?" Pastor Ryder asked as he seated himself behind his desk. He leaned back and crossed one leg up over his other, resting his ankle on his knee. Both hands went behind his head and he stretched out as if relaxing. He was dressed in nice slacks and a shirt, much like some of her teachers wore. His jacket was lying across a nearby chair.

She shrugged. "Fine."

"How's school?" the pastor asked when she didn't volunteer any more.

She blanched. Someone had told him.

"What happened?" her father asked, seeing the look on her face.

"Nothing."

Pastor Ryder dropped his leg and brought his hands to rest on his stomach. "I heard today was talent day," he said casually.

It was her dad's turn to blanch and she was glad. "Today?" He looked at her and she knew what was coming.

She didn't want to hear it. He would apologize because he'd forgotten and then ask her what else they were planning, as if he were going to show up.

The pastor looked from one to the other in confusion, trying to read what was going on. She glared at them both. "I got to read a story I wrote."

"Well, that's great." Pastor Ryder's reply only made her madder, though she was certain he had no idea why. So, she just had to tell him.

"I got detention."

"What?" Her father glared.

"For the story," she explained, and though she tried to act proud that her audience had been shocked and aghast at her story, she hated herself for what she'd done.

"I don't understand." The pastor's gentle gaze made her want to scream. He wasn't angry but did show a need for an explanation. "You didn't read the story?" he asked.

Sarah tilted her chin and said politely, "Yes, I did, but they didn't like the topic."

"And what was the topic, young lady?" her dad asked. He clenched the arms of the chair, bracing himself. Boy, was he mad. His eyes flashed and his voice dropped to nearly a whisper, low and deep. She felt chills touch her spine and wanted to laugh, cry, run. She wasn't sure what she wanted to do, on second thought, since she was suddenly so scared she couldn't move. "My story was about getting rid of the homeless problem."

She saw her dad cast a look at the pastor and then back at her. "The rest of it," he said softly. The softer his voice, the madder he was. She hadn't ever heard him whisper like this.

"I described, in detail, how they could fill up the landfill and then we could cremate them like my mom."

She felt sick over what she'd written, but she had been so mad at her dad.

"You what?" Her father started to stand.

Finding her feet, Sarah jumped up. "Go ahead and yell." Her voice wobbled, so she raised it to cover the fear. "That's all you care about—those people. You didn't care about Mom being gone. You said you were going to change."

Her body trembled and she felt tears sting her eyes. "I hate you! You brought me here away from Mom and then you leave me! I'm all alone!"

Embarrassed that she couldn't stop the tears from falling, she turned and ran out the door.

"Sarah!" Chase called after his daughter and jumped up to follow.

"Let her go," Dakota said.

Chase stopped by the door. Wearily he dropped his forehead against the doorjamb. "Did you hear what she said about killing those people?"

Dakota's chair squeaked as he shifted. "I think it accomplished its purpose."

Chase turned and stared in disbelief at Dakota. "What are you talking about? My daughter is turning into one of those kids from Columbine."

Dakota shook his head. "No, Chase. Sit down."

Chase hesitated, torn. Finally, he walked over and dropped to his chair. "I forgot the talent show today."

Dakota nodded. "And I think that's the real problem." He paused and studied Chase. Finally, he asked, "Why did you come here, Chase?"

Chase rubbed the back of his neck and then tossed his hat into the now-empty chair. "I thought counseling would help Sarah."

"No." Dakota shook his head. "Why did you come here, back to Shenandoah?"

Chase thought back to how life had been before, the hectic schedule and never being home. "I wanted a slower way of life for my daughter, a place where she would be safe now that she doesn't have a mother, a place where she could heal."

Dakota nodded. He didn't say anything for the longest time. He shifted in his chair and crossed his hands over his stomach. "How did she like putting out the things that used to belong to her mom?"

Chase remembered that week he'd finally broken down and put out the memories he'd boxed up. One by one, like fine porcelain, they'd removed homemade picture frames, trinkets and such, as well as the expensive items, and placed them around the house. It had almost killed him, reliving each memory of when Ruth had received the gifts. "She liked it. We had pizza and watched a movie. It was a great time."

"For her?"

"For both of us." Chase rubbed his eyes. "It hurt though, seeing all of those reminders. I lie awake at night wishing my wife was next to me, wanting to hold her, protect her, but I didn't and she's gone."

"You can't protect someone from a disease, Chase," Dakota said softly.

"I promised to love and protect her when I married her," Chase said. "My bed is empty now. My heart is empty and I have a daughter who looks just like her who is hurting and running as fast as she can toward trouble."

"She does look like Ruth, doesn't she?" Dakota agreed.

"So much so it hurts sometimes." Chase's heart squeezed as he thought about it.

"Is that why you're avoiding her?"

"What?" Chase's head jerked up. Anger shot through

him, electrifying every nerve in his body. Sitting up straight, he clenched his hands in defiance. "I'm not avoiding my daughter."

Dakota didn't say anything, simply studied his friend.

Slowly, Chase thought back over the time since his wife had died. "God forgive me, I am, aren't I?"

He had come here to give his daughter more time with him but it hadn't happened. "I'm filling every extra minute of time with overtime and volunteer activities." His heart broke as he realized he was.

Still Dakota said nothing.

"I didn't realize…" A great raspy sob broke forth unexpectedly as he finally reached his limit. Tears he hadn't shed since his wife's death fell as he realized the injustice he'd done his daughter. "I didn't realize that looking at her was like looking at my wife. I didn't know I was doing it."

Dakota sat forward. "And that by avoiding your daughter, you kept bottled up inside you all the pain of your loss."

Chase punched the desk.

Dakota didn't move as things fell off.

Chase grabbed up his hat and crushed it. Slowly he regained a tenuous control. "And now I've lost my daughter, too."

"No, Chase." Dakota's voice was gentle. "You haven't lost your daughter. She still loves you. Do you think she'd be acting out like she has been if she didn't?"

Chase rubbed his eyes, embarrassed over the tears, but unable to stop them completely. "I miss Ruth so much. She was the one who always reached out to

Sarah. She bridged the gap between us, brought us together in the evenings. Dakota, I'm not sure I know how to do that."

"Maybe you should ask Sarah."

"What do you mean?" he asked. Forcing the emotions aside, he took a breath and prayed a prayer that God would help him discover how to help his daughter.

"You're grieving over your loss, Chase. You've kept it bottled up so you could be a parent to Sarah, but it's only kept you apart from her. Confide in Sarah. Let her know you hurt, too. Cry together. Hug each other. When things look dark, communicate with her and ask her what it is that is coming between you."

"She's only a kid," Chase said. He remembered holding her the first day she was born, and when she started crawling, her first smile, first step, first day at school. How proud he had been and how much he'd loved seeing his wife hold their child.

Dakota nodded. "Yeah, she's a kid, and what kid isn't opinionated."

Chase had to agree with that.

"She might not be able to answer your questions," Dakota continued, "but she'll know you care. And then pull out a board game and sit down and play together. Or dot to dot. The activity doesn't matter, the effort does."

"I guess I need to drop the shelter then," Chase said wearily.

Dakota shook his head. "Not necessarily. But ask Sarah if she'd like to help you. She likes woodworking, according to my mom. Or maybe she'd like to paint.

There's still a lot of things to do, so find something to do together. More importantly, ask her. And listen."

Chase sighed. "I haven't been listening. Man, I have to be there to listen." He shook his head. Realizing his hat was a mess, he tossed it back into the empty chair.

"Don't beat yourself up, Chase," Dakota said. "You're grieving and it's a long road. But you and Sarah aren't alone."

Glancing at the door, he said, "I need to go find her. A lot of things have to change between us."

Dakota hurt for his friend but he nodded his understanding. Sarah had been gone long enough that she'd had time to cool down. "It's an ongoing process, brother," Dakota advised him with one last word of advice. "Take it one step at a time. We're all here to help you."

Chase shook his head. "I want to but I just don't know how. Guess I'm going to learn though." He stood and grabbed his slightly out-of-shape hat. "Thanks, Dakota." He started toward the door but paused. Turning back, he asked, "What am I going to do about her story?"

Dakota shrugged. His friend had made great strides today but the road was just starting. He thought how they could use the story with a positive angle. Suddenly he smiled. "Have her write a new one. Maybe you two could brainstorm together."

Chase thought about it and nodded. "Thanks."

He headed out the door just as three men came in.

Dakota looked in surprise as his assistant came rushing in around the three older gentlemen. "I told them you were busy."

Dakota shook his head and straightened up in his

chair. Reaching forward, he moved some papers aside. "It's all right. Chase is just leaving. I can make some time for them."

This did not bode well. Three of the five elders stood before him. Zachary Bennett, the leader, hung behind Odel Baker and Justin Gonzales. Odel wore a long-sleeved shirt and dress jacket with jeans and boots. He was a follower, not a leader, and unfortunately, he'd been following Zach for as long as Dakota could remember. Justin was Spanish-American and owned a large ranch west of town. A good man, but he listened too much to Zach as well. He was in his late fifties, his dark brown hair shot through with silver threads. He was dressed the most casually of the three, wearing jeans, a long-sleeved striped shirt with a bolo tie around his neck. He carried a blue-jean jacket over his arm.

He wondered where Jess Denham and Blaine Geismer were, the other two elders, the only two who would stand up to Zach.

Leaning back in his chair, Dakota crossed his hands over his stomach and mentally braced himself. Offering up a quick prayer for guidance, he nodded toward the chairs. "What can I do for you gentlemen today?"

Odel took a seat in front of him. The oldest of the three, it looked as if he was going to be the spokesman. Odd, considering Zach was the one who usually took control of the elders. "We've had some complaints, Pastor Ryder, about the fact you haven't been spending as much time in church or with church activities."

Dakota should have known this was coming. He had really thought it would blow over, however. He'd been seeing Meghan for a while now and was head over heels in love with her. Obviously, that wasn't public knowledge. But him being seen around town with her and her living out behind his house *was* public knowledge.

Still, he wasn't going to give in so easily to them coming to him about Meghan. He had a right to a private life—and some time off. He knew the whole situation boiled down to the fact that Zach was angry that he didn't have control over him, the young, naive pastor, anymore.

"I'm not sure what you mean," Dakota said innocently. "I'm here my normal business hours."

"That woman," one of the elders muttered from behind Zach.

"Cindy McKinley?" Dakota asked, knowing very well that wasn't who he'd meant. "Yes, I was very happy to see her back in church Sunday." She hadn't been there in a while.

He avoided smiling at the look on Justin's face. Zach scowled, while Odel shook his head. "No. I mean yes, I'm sure it was nice to have her back in church, but we were talking about..." He trailed off and cleared his throat. "Now, son, we understand she's a pretty little thing, but you have the church's reputation to think about."

He frowned as if confused. Of course he wasn't, but these men did irritate him sometimes.

Zach was having none of it. Impatiently, he snapped out, "Meghan O'Halleran. My wife and I told you it wasn't good to be seen with her. It's the rumors. And if that's not bad enough, people are calling this church and getting an answering machine. You're supposed to be here for them. And what about that youth project? Why aren't you heading that up? Suddenly you have no time for that."

Dakota continued to frown. "I haven't heard any rumors." He didn't want to admit how aggravated he was with these three men. They had caused problems from the first day he'd arrived. They felt he was too young, too inexperienced, too whatever, to run such a well-established church. Oh, it'd been couched in, *Let us help train you,* but as they'd realized he wouldn't give in over every circumstance, their fatherly attitudes had turned to resentment.

It didn't look as if the subject of Meghan was going to go away, however. Maybe he'd made a miscalculation in not putting his foot down earlier.

"That's what I have a youth pastor for," Dakota said simply.

Odel, empowered by the support of the other two, added, "You're too worried about one tree to see the forest. And, it seems the young lady has been giving beer to adolescents, namely, that young girl we just saw run out of here as we came in."

Dakota shook his head to deny it. "You'd take a kid's word over the principal's?" He chuckled.

"This isn't a laughing matter. You're grieving the Holy Spirit, Pastor Ryder," said Zach.

Heat flushed Dakota's face—the heat of anger. Zach knew better than that. "Perhaps you'd better look to your own beam first, Zach. You know Meghan has MS and that I'm involved with her. So what if I'm not spending as much time at church. Do you know my prayer life? Do you know when I'm at the hospital? What I'm doing at night?"

"Well, that's not good, either," Justin added in his accented voice. "You won't remember her grandmother well, but she was a handful. Very bitter woman and needed much help."

Odel nodded. "She took up all of her daughter's time. The situation was so bad that eventually the son-in-law left and divorced the daughter. It was a tragic time in their family. And if you're spending time visiting people at the hospital at night, what do you think will happen when you are even more involved with this woman and she needs all your time?"

"Meghan isn't the same as her mother or grandmother," Dakota warned, his voice low. He forced himself not to move a muscle where the vultures could see. If he did, they'd see his anger, see that his hands shook. Quickly he prayed quietly that God would help him calm down and try to keep their words in perspective. They didn't have supreme power over him. God did. And if Dakota kept his eyes on God, not men, things would be okay.

"Maybe she isn't her mother or grandmother, but the disease is the same," Zach said dismissively. "You say you're called to be a pastor and yet you're so busy with this woman who takes up most of your time that the people of this church are suffering."

"But she is a member of this church now," Dakota argued, feeling his temper rise once again. "And name one person besides those in this office who has been complaining?"

"We can't divulge names," Zach said superiorly, which was, of course, the only excuse Zach could use, and not a good one, to keep information from him.

"What does my private life have to do with my job as pastor?" Dakota decided to take a different tack.

Zach looked aghast at Dakota's question. "How can you even ask that? Your moral obligation to this church is obvious."

"My moral obligation to God obviously isn't," he muttered loud enough for them all to hear.

"What's going on here?"

Ah. Blaine Geismer and Jess Denham came into the office, looking put out and out of breath, but there. Blaine's white hair was windblown, his white shirt askew, as if he'd dressed hurriedly. Jess, in his forties and the newest elder, looked plain mad, his dark hair covered by the baseball cap he still wore.

As if realizing he still had it on his head, he suddenly jerked it off.

Zach scowled while Justin frowned. Odel shrank in his chair at the confrontation.

Dakota leaned back in his chair and did his best to appear calm. "It seems I've been the topic of discussion lately at many a dinner table, gentlemen," he told the two other elders who obviously hadn't been informed of this meeting, if the looks they were tossing at the other three men were any indication.

He'd bet his assistant had called them, bless her heart.

"Well, now—" Blaine actually flushed as he tried to joke "—is that anything abnormal?"

Dakota chuckled because it really wasn't. It seemed pastors were fair game for anyone who didn't like what they said that Sunday.

Zach broke in. "This isn't a time for levity, Blaine. The pastor's moral code is being called into question. He's taken to skipping workdays, taking time off to go gallivanting around the county and ignoring church members' calls."

Dakota didn't deny a thing. What could he say when they were determined to accuse him without producing accusers?

"If this persists," Justin said to Blaine and Jess, "we will have to ask for his resignation."

Dakota sat forward, stunned that they would go that far. A slow fury built. "If you want to ask for my resignation, you'll have to bring it before the church, and I think the church will support *me* in this. Speaking of which, if you can't see the vision of this church, perhaps I should be asking for *your* resignations."

Shouting erupted. From all five men.

Zach was clearly infuriated, but no more than Dakota.

It was Jess who regained control of the situation first. "No one is going to be asking for the pastor's resignation. We're here to support him and to help make sure this church is run biblically."

Dakota felt properly chastised by Jess's words. Not for being in love with Meghan, but for being so angry at the audacity of Zach, Justin and Odel.

"Biblically?" Zach scoffed. "Do you call it biblical when he shirks his duties? Mark my words. This is going to destroy the church. A house divided won't stand." Zach stormed out.

Justin started out as well but paused at the door. "Think about what you're doing, Ryder." Then he turned and left.

Odel slunk out, not meeting anyone's eyes.

When they were gone, Jess and Blaine turned back

to Dakota. "Is she a Christian, Dakota?" Jess asked bluntly. "We know about the time away from church, and that a woman will take more of your time. Not that we find that bad, but we need some details if we're going to counter what Zach and his supporters are saying."

Dakota nodded. "She's asking about baptism, as well. She asked Jesus into her heart a few weeks ago. She shines now. She has such a tender and exciting interest in everything about God. She's searching and growing by leaps and bounds." He suddenly realized he'd been going on and on about Meghan, and so he stopped.

Blaine sighed and rubbed the back of his neck. "We weren't informed about Zach's desire to reprimand you, obviously, though we knew the elders weren't happy that you were interested in this woman. Do you understand the disease she has? I know I don't, but, well, I mean, have you prayed about it? Are you sure this isn't going to interfere with your calling?"

Dakota resented the question, but realized they were simply concerned. He sighed. "I have done nothing but pray about it. I will admit I haven't been putting in as many hours at the church, but honestly, I do feel that God sent Meghan my way for a reason. I'd gotten off track. Yes, I'm a pastor, but my relationship with God had been suffering. Seeing through her eyes, things are getting back to where they should be. I'm sorry if it means less hours here, but God, not this church, has to be first in my life."

Blaine sighed. "You're overworked, Pastor."

Jess nodded his agreement.

Blaine continued, "As for Meghan, I'm glad for you

if it's God's plan, brother, but there are three elders who are going to challenge you. Think hard about what you're considering with this woman. It could cause a church split."

Dakota wondered what had been going on with his life lately. He had been so busy with *things* and doing certain acts, that he hadn't really taken the time he needed just to be with God, until Meghan had shown up and pointed out how busy he'd been *doing* instead of *serving*. How had his life gotten so busy that he'd forgotten God? That was why Meghan had come into his life. She had shown him, in her own gentle way, that he needed time with God, in peace and quiet, because his relationship with the Creator was more important than the creation.

Silently he thanked God for the wonderful woman He had sent his way to balance out his life, which had been out of control until now. And then he vowed, starting right now, that things were going to change.

"Dakota!" Chase came running into the office, interrupting their conversation. Alarmed, Dakota stood.

"I can't find Sarah. I've looked everywhere. She didn't come back in here, did she?"

"She hasn't been in here. Wait," he said as Chase turned to leave. "What happened?"

Chase paused and turned back. "I went to talk to Sarah after our discussion and she wasn't out there by the truck waiting like I thought she'd be. I checked around the building, in all of the classrooms. I can't find her."

Dakota frowned. "Maybe she walked back to my mom's. Let me call and see if she's there."

Chase nodded.

As Dakota picked up the phone, he could only hope their problems would be solved that easily.

Chapter Nineteen

"That was Dakota."

Carolyne hung up the phone and turned toward Meghan, who had just walked in. She was on her cane again today, exhausted and looking every bit the part of a disabled person. She hated to tell Meghan all that had transpired, but she needed to know.

Meghan smiled, as she did any time Dakota's name was mentioned. "What did he have to say?"

Carolyne motioned to a chair.

Meghan's smile faded as she took a seat.

"It seems three of the elders of the church have put pressure on Dakota about his relationship with you."

Meghan flushed. "We don't have a relationship."

Carolyne looked at her askance.

"Not exactly," she whispered, correcting herself.

"At any rate, the other elders showed up and stopped the discussion."

Meghan gripped her hands in worry. "This is all my fault. I shouldn't have come here."

"Ridiculous." Carolyne waved a hand. "God sent you here. Some things simply need cleaning out," she said mysteriously to Meghan. Carolyne felt that Meghan was making her son take notice of some dead weight in the church. "And we need your expertise at the shelter. Meghan, your presence has given me new life and new direction. And that is because God sent you here."

Carolyne moved forward and took Meghan's hands. "Don't let the enemy convince you otherwise. You are a treasure sent by God. You've turned this town upside down and made us all take a fresh look at life through your eyes."

Meghan glanced down awkwardly. "I don't understand how."

"That's how God works, honey."

She released her hands. "There's more."

Meghan glanced up worriedly.

The sound of the knocker on the front door sounded.

Carolyne frowned. "Who could that be?"

"Is this bad news?" Meghan asked and got up to follow Carolyne.

"It just might be."

She pulled open the door and found Mary and Margaret, both very agitated, standing there. "Dear, we just heard on the scanner! It's terrible. Simply terrible."

"We wanted to know if we could do anything," Margaret added.

"What?" Meghan demanded, alarmed.

Carolyne sighed. Turning toward Meghan, she said, "Chase's daughter is missing. Dakota had hoped she was on her way here from their meeting. She was upset."

Meghan blanched. "We've got to find her."

Carolyne nodded.

"Can we cook some soup or make some bread? Maybe some cookies for Sarah?" Mary asked worriedly.

Carolyne took the time to reassure the sisters. "That would be wonderful. I'm sure Chase would appreciate it."

"Apple doesn't fall far from the tree," Margaret muttered. "Riding his bike through our yard and now his daughter running wild." She tsked. "Come, sister. Let's get to work."

Mary paused. "If you need anything else, call. And please phone us when you find her."

They turned to leave.

"Can you keep an eye on our house? If you see her, contact the sheriff." Carolyne added.

Margaret nodded and Mary hurriedly tottered off after her.

Carolyne shut the door.

"What are we going to do?" Meghan asked, already heading toward the back door.

"I suppose we can get in the car and drive the streets between here and the church. Maybe she's headed this way."

They hurried out to Carolyne's car. Once inside, Carolyne started it and backed out.

Meghan was frantic, Carolyne realized. "I'm worried about her. Too many things happen out on the streets."

"You're speaking from firsthand experience, aren't you?" Carolyne asked, knowing very well that she was.

Meghan nodded. Her eyes were already scanning desperately for any sign of the young girl. "I've come to care for Sarah," she whispered.

Carolyne smiled as she eased around the corner

slowly so they could search all the yards as they drove. "She's family now."

Meghan didn't say anything, simply kept wringing her hands. Carolyne didn't admit how telling that action was. Finally, Meghan whispered, "I care for Dakota, too."

Carolyne turned down the next street. "Which is why you can't leave. If you ever tried to leave, I'm afraid my son would hunt for you until he found you."

Meghan didn't comment, so Carolyne added quietly, "He loves you, you know."

"I love him," she finally whispered then added, "I was so afraid something like this would happen. I didn't want it to, because of my grandmother. I remember her."

Carolyne felt her heart break as she saw the struggle going on in Meghan.

"My dad left my mom. It tore our family apart."

Carolyne nodded. "But you have to trust God. He brought you to us, honey."

Meghan shook her head. Turning, she looked at Carolyne, temporarily forgetting to search the street. "You have been so accepting of me, and I wouldn't hesitate to accept Dakota's, uh…um…" She blushed, hoping Carolyne hadn't caught what she was about to say. "I'm the cause of problems for him. If we continue on, it's not going to get better. I know now my disease doesn't matter, but then it does. I am going to take time away from his congregation."

Carolyne slowed the car to a stop at a stoplight. Looking at Meghan, she said, "I'm going to tell you something that few people know." She took a breath and then let it out.

"I'm a murderer."

Meghan gaped.

Carolyne nodded. "Mary and Margaret know of the incident, as did my husband." Her gaze took on a far-off look. "I used to be very judgmental of people. Many Christians get into that boat. They look at the outside of someone. That person doesn't dress right. Or that person smells. That person is ugly or fat or a smart aleck. Oh, we can get caught up about so many things. That person drinks or smokes, and the list goes on and on. We're real good at labeling people."

Carolyne remembered painfully the ordeal she was relating. "When I was first married I worked a short time in a malt shop. It was a pharmacy of sorts." She smiled, remembering that store. "Someone came into the place I worked one day. I thought she was drunk. She stumbled around. I had nothing but disdain for her. I was very young. I'd only been married a year and my husband had mentioned to me I shouldn't be so judgmental. But I refused to listen. When that woman came into the little dime store, I ignored her until she insisted she wanted something. I suggested she needed to leave. She wasn't talking right, confusing her words and such. But she wouldn't leave. She even grabbed at me. Well, I wasn't going to be accosted by a drunk, so I called the manager and told him she was getting violent.

"He didn't question me. I had a sterling reputation, you see. He had her ejected."

Carolyne watched Meghan very carefully. "That

night, the sheriff came by to question me about the woman. You see, she was dead. Later, an autopsy revealed she was a diabetic. She hadn't been drunk at all, but in need of help."

Meghan gasped.

Carolyne nodded. "If I had stopped to really look at this woman, see her inside and not what appeared on the outside, I would have realized she needed help."

Carolyne started driving again. "And those elders at church, they're murderers, too. They murder people every day with their judgmental attitude, refusing to see like Jesus sees. Dakota isn't like them. He let them control him for a while, but because of you, he's beginning to see that God is what is important, not people's small-minded picture of the church."

"I've been trying to make decisions for Dakota instead of allowing him to make his own decisions," Meghan whispered. "Just like those elders. I have been deciding that because of my disease and the possible future problems Dakota shouldn't be with me."

She nodded. "You have to see you and Dakota how God sees you, honey—as someone special. We don't know why God calls us, how He calls us, we simply know that when He brings us together in love we need to let Him work."

Suddenly a flash of something caught Meghan's eye. Meghan grabbed Carolyne's arm. "Stop! Go back. Turn at that street."

Carolyne hit the brakes, causing Meghan to fly forward. "What did you see?"

Meghan braced her hand against the dashboard and glanced back toward the street they'd just passed. "I think I saw a few blocks down near the warehouses a pink coat on a young girl."

"Sarah has a pink coat." Carolyne quickly backed up and turned right, down the deserted street.

Meghan watched intently. "There!" She pointed. "Past the garbage bin. Call Dakota."

Carolyne pulled to a stop as close as she could get.

Sarah spotted them and started to run.

Meghan shoved open the door.

"Wait." Carolyne jerked at her purse for her cell phone and started dialing her son.

Meghan shook her head. Grabbing her cane, she called out, "Sarah. Sarah! Stop right there, young lady!"

Moving as fast as she could with her cane, she maneuvered around the heaps of trash. This had once been an industrial complex that was now run-down and abandoned. Even as she moved around pieces of rotting wood toward the opposite end of the alleyway, she saw a rat run past.

"I don't want to wait," Sarah called out.

Meghan tripped over something. She caught her balance and rubbed at her eyes. She hadn't seen that piece of wood, she realized, and saw it was fuzzy as well. The stress of the last week and especially today was unbelievable. She shook her head. "I don't care what you want—" Meghan started then changed her mind. "Well, I do care, but not about running away."

Sarah shifted from foot to foot, her pink coat zipped tight against the wind. Meghan hadn't gotten her coat out of the car, and the wind stung her exposed arms, chilling them to the bone.

"No you don't. No one does!"

Meghan almost stepped on something and realized she hadn't seen it again. Sighing in frustration, she side-stepped the trash and continued. She had gotten nearly to the opposite end of the alleyway. Glancing back, she could see Carolyne on the phone. Good. Dakota could handle this.

"You're wrong, Sarah, honey," Meghan said softly. The young girl had been crying. "I wouldn't be caught dead out on a street like this except for you, because once upon a time I lived on a street like this."

"Oh, poor you," Sarah said, trying to sound mean but glancing around uneasily as she said it. She shrugged. "Nothing is here."

"I guess you missed the rat." Meghan stopped a few feet away from Sarah. "Anyway, why don't you tell me what's going on here."

Sarah lifted her chin mutinously and crossed her arms.

Meghan glared at her. "That look won't work on me. I used it myself a few times. I know exactly what it means."

"Oh yeah?"

Kids, she thought, and sighed. "Look, honey, you're not really mad at me. Why don't you tell me where you're going."

Sarah shrugged and looked away. "A friend hangs out here."

Meghan felt cold chills. Absently she rubbed her eyes. She had a bad feeling. What was the name of that girl, the one who'd given her beer? "Jesse?" she asked.

Startled, Sarah gaped.

Bingo. She'd hit the jackpot.

"Well, at least she cares," Sarah said.

Slowly, Meghan shook her head. "I doubt that. If she cared, she wouldn't be giving you beer. Or inviting you into neighborhoods like this."

Sarah swelled up as if to say something, but Meghan took the lead. "Your dad was worried sick when he realized you were gone."

"He hates me," Sarah argued and fresh tears filled her eyes. "I don't want to be with him anymore."

"Oh please, Sarah." Meghan resisted the urge to roll her eyes. Then more gently, she added, "Life can be rough, especially when you lose your mom."

"What would you know about that?" Sarah asked, not believing she had any experience in that area.

"I had a rotten grandmother and because of her, my dad left us. Not long after that, I lost my mom. I ended up in a foster home. I know what it's like to lose parents. And they weren't Christian like your dad. My mom was an alcoholic."

"Like you?" Sarah said nastily.

Meghan sighed. "Like I almost was, yes," Meghan agreed. "I had started down the wrong path, angry and hurt over my losses, but it took people like Dakota and Ms. Carolyne to show me the right direction. Don't go down that road, Sarah. There's nothing but loss there."

Meghan shifted, feeling suddenly tired. Wearily, she rubbed her neck. "I was lucky I didn't end up dead when I was living on the streets. I don't remember much of that time, to be honest, because of the alcohol. You'll end up hurt or worse—dead—if you keep going that way. Trust me on this."

"What makes you so smart about that?" Sarah's voice had changed from defiant to little girl. She didn't want to believe Meghan, but Meghan could see in Sarah's eyes that she was wavering about running away.

If she could only think of a way to convince her without Sarah feeling as if she'd given in.

"Hey there, girl." The loud drunk voice came from Meghan's left.

Sarah's eyes widened as a teenage boy, covered in dirt and grime, staggered out, a bottle in his hand. He had long hair that hung in limp, greasy strands and his jeans hung way down on his hips.

Sarah backed up. The boy was looking right at her. "You come to join the party? It's a block over, honey. Come let papa show you the way."

Meghan recognized the lust in his eyes and her stomach turned. "Sarah," Meghan said sharply and the child ran to her, getting behind her.

For the first time the youth noticed Meghan. His gaze ran up and down her before turning ugly. "Leave the kid alone. If she wants to play, let her play."

"Go to Carolyne. Now," Meghan ordered.

She heard Sarah's feet take off.

The youth started forward. Meghan lifted her cane and swung it at him.

He grabbed the end of it and jerked her forward.

His breath stank as he caught her up against him. "Well, looks like you want to play instead," he whispered, and she could smell the stale stench of cigarettes and alcohol on him.

"Not likely," she muttered and pushed back, trying to regain her footing.

The boy laughed and ran his hand down her back, fondling her.

She gasped and slapped at him. "Leave me alone."

He glared at her and pulled her closer. "Whacha gonna do if I don't?"

Meghan had not been so terrified as when she'd been grabbed by the man in the shelter. *God, I need help,* she silently prayed. She didn't know if He would hear her or not, but she had to try.

Fight or flight kicked in and she started struggling.

That only made the young man laugh harder.

When she realized her actions encouraged him, she decided her only option was to hurt him where she could. When he pulled at her again, she lifted her knee as hard and fast as she could.

The boy sucked in a breath and with violence she didn't know someone so small could have, he grabbed her and threw her across the alley.

Her back hit the wall and she bounced, literally, from the wall onto a bunch of old rotting cardboard boxes.

The young boy cursed and started toward her, limping. "I'm going to kill you for that."

He pulled out a switchblade.

She suddenly realized the blade was fuzzy and was certain it was her way of protecting herself by blocking it out. She closed her eyes.

And then he was there, the blade arcing down.

Chapter Twenty

Dakota sailed through the air, seeing the knife closing in on Meghan's crumpled form. Never in his life had he been as terrified as he was at that moment.

But he knew that if he could stop this youth from stabbing Meghan, a knife in his own gut would be worth it.

His body met with the boy's shoulder and they both went rolling into the cardboard boxes.

Chase came from nowhere, kicking the boy's hand. The youth cried out.

With a vicious twist, Chase grabbed the youth's hand and flipped him over, knocking Dakota out of the way.

Dakota didn't argue as this was Chase's area of expertise.

"Dakota!" Carolyne cried out from the other end of the street. Dakota glanced up and nodded as he pulled himself to his feet and rushed to Meghan.

"Daddy!" Sarah called out. She was crying and in Carolyne's arms.

Meghan was still lying in the boxes, her dress hitched up to her knees, her legs covered in grime from where she'd fallen.

He knelt down next to her. "Sweet Meghan."

It was all he could say. Not waiting to see if she was okay, he hauled her up into his arms and held her closely. "What were you thinking? You scared me to death! I nearly died when I saw that guy attacking you."

"Where did you come from?" Her body trembled though she clung to him for dear life. "I couldn't let him hurt Sarah. He would have."

"Shush," Dakota said, hearing the fear in her voice. "I'm sorry. I didn't mean to chastise you." He hugged her tighter. "We got a call from Mom and were at the end of the alley just as you hit that kid with your cane."

Dakota rocked her back and forth. "One of the bravest things I've seen, though by the time we got out of the car and started toward you, he'd already pulled that knife."

"Dakota," Meghan whispered into his shoulder.

He shook his head. "No, it's okay," he said softly. "You're fine. I can't tell you what it felt like seeing you in danger. Oh, Meghan, Meghan," he whispered, realizing he was shaking. He heard Chase reading the rights to Meghan's attacker and he saw that other squad cars had pulled up, but still he didn't release Meghan. Instead, he said, "I couldn't have lived if you had been killed. I can't tell you how terrified I was. You see—"

"Dakota," Meghan whispered again but he ignored her.

"Hear me out, sweet Meghan. I love you."

She stilled in his arms.

"I want you to marry me. Since you've come into my life, I've changed, for the better. God has changed my outlook on life and you have become such an integral part, I don't think I could live without you."

"But what about the church?" Her voice was small and worried.

He ran his hand through her hair. "I am a pastor and in charge of this church, but I'm a man, too, and God has blessed us with marriage, you know."

"But the MS—"

He squeezed her tighter. "We'll deal with it when it acts up. That's part of your life, and it will be part of my life, as well."

"No, you don't understand," she started.

"Meghan—" Dakota hugged her tighter "—Meghan, my love, I do understand. Some of the people at the church want me to spend every waking minute at their disposal. That's not what God called me to do. He's called me to preach the Word, instruct the flock and love them, not be their slave. I don't know how things happened, but things are going back like they should be. And the best way for that to happen is for me to keep my priorities straight. And I can't think of anyone better than you to keep me in line when I get off track. God sent you here—that is, unless you don't want me," Dakota said, suddenly unsure.

He sat back to look at her.

She was staring off into the distance, at him, but through him. "Meghan?"

She bit her lip. "I love you, Dakota, and would love to marry you, but…"

When she didn't say anything, he studied her face. "What is it?"

"I think I'm having an MS attack. Can someone go blind from MS?"

Dakota felt his heart drop to his feet. "Chase? Chase! We need to get Meghan to the hospital!"

He stood and lifted her into his arms. "I thought you were scared and worried about my proposal!" he said as he made his way down the alley.

Meghan sighed. "I am scared and worried, but well, not about that."

He got to Chase's car and sat her in the back seat, sliding in with her. Chase was just putting the prisoner in one of the squad cars. He finished and hurried over.

"What's the matter?" Chase bent down to examine Meghan.

Dakota shook his head. "MS attack. She's lost her sight."

Chase looked surprised but didn't argue. He hurried over to his daughter and then returned, jumping into the car and taking off, leaving Sarah with Dakota's mom.

"I'm sorry," Meghan whispered.

Dakota pulled her close. "For what?"

"This. If you want to take back your proposal, I'd understand."

Chase looked up sharply into the rearview mirror.

Dakota pointedly ignored the look. "Never, sweet Meghan. I want you to spend the rest of your life with me."

Meghan held on to him and he hugged her close. "I don't know if my vision will come back. I don't know if it's even from the MS. Can you accept that? What am I saying? I don't know if I can." She hesitated. "I'm scared," she whispered.

Dakota rocked her. "Sweetheart, if you were in a wheelchair or bedridden, I'd accept it because I love you."

"Oh, Dakota." Meghan buried her head in his shoulder.

"Jesus, heal her," Dakota whispered over her.

She shuddered.

He repeated the prayer again and again.

In minutes they were at the hospital. As Dakota got out, a stretcher was brought out for Meghan.

Laying her on it, he leaned down next to her ear. "I'll be waiting out here for an answer, that's how sure I am I want you. No matter what, honey. Now, go get taken care of, okay?"

Meghan reached out for his hand.

He caught her fingers.

She squeezed them. "I can answer you now but I'd rather be able to see you to answer."

He lifted her fingers to his cheek. "I love you, sweet Meghan. I can wait."

She shook her head. "I love you, too, Dakota. I think I probably always have." He could see the fear and yet the determined courage as she reached up with her other hand and pulled him closer. "My answer is yes."

She felt for his face and he allowed himself to break into a broad smile. Relief colored her features and tears slipped from her eyes, trickling away into her hairline.

"Pastor, we need to take her now," a hospital attendant said.

He stepped back. "You'll be fine," he called.

She nibbled her lip and clasped her hands, terrified but brave, too. "With God," she called back.

He'd never been so proud.

Chase walked up to him.

"She said yes."

He nodded. "So what are you going to do about your church?"

Dakota frowned. "I have to have some time to pray. Be there on Sunday morning and you'll see."

Chapter Twenty-One

Sunday
Two weeks later

Church had gone well. They had just finished the altar call. Dakota smiled at Meghan, who sat in the first row with his mom. Then he looked out at the expectant crowd.

Normally, right now he would dismiss with prayer. But after two weeks of prayer and that first week at the hospital with Meghan, who had indeed gotten some of her vision back, he had come to a decision.

Meghan was very swollen from prednisone therapy, her face all puffy and red. She had worried about coming with him this morning, but he felt it important she be there, even at her worst, when he made this announcement. Her hands and feet looked awful and her dress was a bit tight on her in the waist, but the doctor said in a week or two that'd be gone. It was all water weight. The best news, however, was that hopefully, in six months she'd have all of her vision back. They'd just have to wait and see. MS was evidently a disease like that, waiting and seeing—a study in patience—something he had learned since meeting Meghan.

"I know you expect me to dismiss you, but I have an announcement to make," he said to the congregation.

His eyes connected with the elders who were unhappy with him and he could tell Zach knew what was coming. Zach stiffened and looked over to where Meghan and Dakota's mom sat.

"I've been pastor here for a while and I hear all the jokes you guys make about my lack of marriage and my living at the church. Well, today things are changing because I have asked Meghan O'Halleran to be my wife and she has accepted."

Gasps went up from the congregation. Some clapped, some gaped, while others cheered.

A few saw two of the elders get up and walk out. Three other families followed suit. Odel didn't leave, though, nor did Jess or Blaine.

His heart grieved as he saw the angered looks on the faces of the ones who'd left. Maybe they'd come back, but that was between them and God.

"Dear heavenly Father," Dakota said, bowing his head and letting everyone fall quiet. *"Bless us today and protect us as we head to our homes. Keep us safe and in an attitude of worship of You. In Jesus' name, amen."*

The pianist started playing.

Meghan stood.

Many rushed forward to congratulate him. He made his way to Meghan's side and slowly down the aisle, taking Meghan with him. "I saw some leave," she whispered as they worked their way to the back door.

He nodded. "It hurts."

She hugged her arm around him.

"It was a lot of tithers that left, your mom said."

He shrugged. "God will provide. It's His church."

Meghan stared up at Dakota. "What a change for a man who has to be in control of everything and constantly busy."

The other elders walked up, so Meghan fell quiet. "My dear," Blaine said, taking her hand. "We are so very happy for this man. I think he has made an excellent choice."

She blushed and Dakota smiled. Jess kissed her hand and Dakota cleared his throat.

Then Odel walked up. Dakota shook his hand.

Odel shifted from foot to foot and then said, "You know, an associate pastor might be out for the short term, but next time the subject is brought up, I'll see to getting you some help."

Dakota smiled warmly. "Thank you, Odel. I appreciate that."

"We can't afford it right now," Jess joked, "but to that end, we have drawn up a plan to involve the elders and deacons more in the daily activities of the church. We had a meeting during the week and made some calls—and we all want to help take over some of the lesser things that you shouldn't have to worry over. It is biblical, after all."

Humbled, Dakota thanked them. "I've been too controlling myself, and never realized I was robbing you of some of the joy of serving."

"That's right, brother," Jess said. "Robbing us of blessings you were."

Everyone laughed.

Blaine turned serious. "It'll be rough for a while, but we've all been around long enough, son, to tell you that God is in control."

"And I know that now," Dakota said, grinning.

"I love you, you know." Megan told him.

Dakota grinned and squeezed her. "Everything will work out."

"What about Chase and Sarah?" she asked.

Dakota drew a finger down the side of her cheek. "I know they're having problems, but I just have this feeling that things are going to work out."

"Oh?"

He smiled. "When God is in control, things work out. And God has some special plans for Chase."

As they left, Dakota turned to Meghan. "Do you still believe in miracles?"

She nodded and hugged his waist. "How could I not? He brought back a friend when I needed him, and gave me His love as well as the love of that best friend."

"So, like Chase, my dear love, God is in control and has some special plans for us," Dakota said, smiling at her.

Meghan leaned up and touched her lips to his cheek. "That sounds intriguing. I can't wait to find out what they are."

"Well, it all started when He brought you to me," Dakota said and returned the gentle kiss.

"No, my love, it started when He brought me home to you."

* * * * *

Dear Reader,

I was diagnosed with MS in 2002. Unlike Meghan, I went to the Web to research the disease and find out more about it. I was excited by what I found because when I had been in the medical field, there was nothing they could do for the disease. However, now they can slow the progression. No, there's no cure, but I believe there will be one day with the strides that have been made.

This book deals with learning the lesson that God is in control. It was something Meghan and Dakota had to learn. And anyone who gets too busy with work or comes down with a devastating medical problem needs to learn the lesson, as well. Let go and praise God because He is in control!

I hope you enjoy the story, and if you want more information on MS, try some of the Web sites I like to visit: www.mswatch.com, www.multiplesclerosis.com or www.msaa.org or the National Multiple Sclerosis Society page. God bless!

You can also visit my Web site for more links at: www.cherylwolverton.com or e-mail if you have questions at: Cheryl@cherylwolverton.com. You can write to me at P.O. Box 106, Faxon, OK 73540.

I look forward to chatting with you!

Cheryl Wolverton

AMAZING LOVE

BY

MAE NUNN

Claire Savage learned not to trust at a young age, and had no use for former rocker Luke Dawson. She didn't expect his noble spirit to soothe her, yet could his gentle touch curb her mistrust when his past resurfaced to threaten them both?

Texas Treasures: These gems from the Lone Star State are strong of heart and strong of faith.

Don't miss AMAZING LOVE
On sale February 2006

Available at your favorite retail outlet.

Steeple Hill®

LIALMN

TITLES AVAILABLE NEXT MONTH

Don't miss these four stories in February

A HANDFUL OF HEAVEN by Jillian Hart
The McKaslin Clan

Hardworking single mother Paige McKaslin was the backbone that held her family together, but when the family diner burned down, it left her free to discover her own path…and a blossoming relationship with rancher Evan Thornton. Could it be that God still had some surprises in store for her?

AMAZING LOVE by Mae Nunn
Texas Treasures

Texas beauty Claire Savage learned a hard lesson the day her father left to pursue his selfish dreams. She never expected church newcomer and former rocker Luke Dawson's noble spirit to soothe her, yet could even his gentle touch curb her mistrust when his past resurfaced to threaten them both?

A MOTHER'S PROMISE by Ruth Scofield
Part of the NEW BEGINNINGS miniseries

A fresh start was hard for single mom Lisa Marley. Though she'd made her share of mistakes, all she wanted was a chance to raise her daughter. Widower Ethan Vance's deepening interest might just be the tie to bind them together…as a family.

CHANGING HER HEART by Gail Sattler
Men of Praise

When lovely Lacey Dachin signed on at the shop next door, it looked as if Randy Reynolds had found a potential lunch date…until she discovered his party-boy past. With his life in stand-up shape, the only thing that needed changing now was Lacey's mind.

LICNM0106